TOWN OF FICTION

To the funniest men alive

[signature]

THE ATLANTIS COLLECTIVE

[signatures]
Aideen Henry
Máire T. Robinson.

ORIGINAL WRITING

978-1-906018-94-8

A CIP catalogue for this book is available from the National Library.

Published by Original Writing Ltd., Dublin, 2009.

Printed by Cahills, Dublin.

Acknowledgements

The Atlantis Collective owe thanks to NUIG's MA in Writing class of 2008; Adrian Frazier; Dearbhla Mooney; Jonathan Williams; Michael Harding. Special thanks to Páraic, Vicki and all at the Galway Arts Centre; Maureen and all at *Cúirt*; Massimo; Michael O'Grady; Deirdre McCurry; Bad Dog Design; and most especially to John Kenny who, as always, allowed himself to be dragged far beyond the call of duty.

Dedicated Follower of Fashion

A thought crossed his mind as the truck struck:
wrong day for frilly pink panties.

by CONOR MONTAGUE

Contents

Editor's Backword

Lamina

by JOHN KENNY

A ram no one seemed to own or want to own roamed in and out of town during all that time.

A full five years.

He moved down the long acres of lanes and byways, in and out of gaps and gateways, up over hills and along by all rivers, front roads, back roads. Straight and in circles. Every source to town.

The old blindly wanted him back so were silent, the young all differed in forecast. He's coming this way. He's coming for you. No. Coming. For you. No for you. No, for you. No. You. Yes. He's coming for you.

Talking not to each other.

His wool draped, raked off his back and belly and fat splattered tail, and the scuffed hairs of his humped black head could be seen here and there where he jumped fences or broke into homesteads and lay for a night, butting low against shed walls in sleep.

Even barbed wire could not hold him those summers.

Far from safe, and only most would escape unhurt.

For some, surrounded.

Beginning of all trouble.

No getting away.

In the wood, under the sun and moon, the beautiful woman shuttled her loom. She rose, and with her distaff drove all other beasts aside when he came. Right through them he paraded.

She readied him for five days and nights in the outhouse.

Then it was time.

Go for them now.

Only one place he did not go on his way. Graveyard. Though the walls were well breached by secret night-time drinkers and lovers, he ripped and ate just the verges, would not pick the lush of the unkept plots. Straight and in circles, he cropped his way slow, relentless as forever, hungry as now.

They are in two. So take them in two.

He moved in on the first group when they thought they were looking.

Puffing their way through their ten-packs, quick lunch just behind them, they were putting off going back up the town. Next class could wait.

Gathered in the pub shed. Amusements. Had forsaken the table-tops and were all at the standing machines, crowded round the one who could fight.

Focused. Highest scores. Beating personal bests.

On the first machine he banished all invaders of space, mother ship safe home every time.

Better again. Chalk it up.

It was on the next machine it happened.

Pac-Man was chewing the maze, gobbling fruit, eating dots and his wandering ghosts, heading for high, when his attention gave. For just that one beat he had heard something new in the tale being told, which always was told, of the time they found the torn mag on the pitch. Of the tits on the cover and sizes and positions within.

Something. Just that one second. And he lost his life.

Swallowed. Game over.

No curse. Not aloud. Such new stories are not to be told.

He just stepped away quiet and went with their noise round him up town. Back up to their own past the girls'.

He moved in on the second group when they were looking at each other.

They were doing their manners.

Sit straight. Straighten skirts.

Not that way, this.

Words are food, chew properly once. Not cud. Around the rugged rock. Three grey geese in a green field grazing. Imagine an imaginary menagerie manager imagining managing an imaginary menagerie. Squeeze and bite down on those vowels.

But all sounds float above what happened at lunchtime PE when hail of basketballs and volleyballs cleared so all could turn.

To see.

Her.

There.

Not the first of them all to bleed, but the first who had not been helped know.

Cruelty and confusion, until Miss took her roughly by the shoulder to the equipment room, told all to change in, waited, then took her gently with whispers to get clean.

Couldn't really even be taken home.

But wherever she is now, is not here, and so sideways looks meet each other, not her.

They wonder, all looks, if such stories are to be talked but not told.

So keep practising that talking.

Again and again, during that time, he took them two by two in this way.

The sane among the old smiled on, struck happy by the parade they could see now.

Others frowned, pointed to thievery, tramps, pub-fights, broken hearts and car crashes, bullies, deadly dares, deaths, baffled solitaries, beaten families.

Had to blame. Lock them or him up.

At last he surely will go.

He will stop breaking through.

But the souse of a town butcher who took to the pub in heroics after roping him at last one evening and hanging him up and slicing his throat drowned later that night inside himself from drink.

The local boy who readied the cutting board and sharpened the boning knife had his eyes scalded out the following day when the skinning hose turned on him.

The half-touched woman who took the shop over soon closed for good because even the big new freezers she put in could not stop the smell.

Where the raw meat was finally buried in the old quarry dogs circled and pawed silently at thin crusted ground all night all winter.

When the frosts fell off in early springtime hair and wool hung along the briars and thorns of the ditches and hedges of the fields which are everywhere.

In the Beginning

by PATRICIA BYRNE

Day begins. As it is in the beginning of each of her days she will awaken to bird song at dawn. This is a day, the first Friday of the month – that she will start by mouthing a novena verse:

> *Give help to your people, O Lord*
> *in their time of distress*
> *and comfort them in their sorrows.*

It is the blackbirds that make the dawn song, the blackbirds that frighten birds from the feeder at the front window of the yellow pebble-dashed bungalow. Later, she will watch a goldfinch hop on to the feeder and nibble. She will notice the swipe of yellow on its wings and blotches of red at the side of its head. It will remind her of buttercups and beetroot.

It is a day that the light will press through the bronze curtains and reveal lines on her face from nine decades of living – lines like the dry, cracked surface of the peat at Riasc bog beyond the house. She will mumble her morning prayers:

> *... never was it known that anyone who fled to thy protection,*
> *implored thy help and sought thy intercession was left unaided ...*
> *despise not my petitions, but in thy clemency hear and answer me.*

It is a day she will drag her legs from under the bed-clothes, push herself on to her elbow, lift one, then two legs on to the crimson and yellow lino. Step by step she will move to the commode in the corner of the room, hair-net flopping over one ear. Sitting, she will worry about the effort of rising again.

Soon the back bedroom will be bathed in yellow light. The

distant spire of the church of Saint Margaret Mary Alacoque will rise outside in black silhouette against the morning sky.

The cemetery close to the church has a vantage point on the valley and the yellow house below. Sometimes, in the winter, she had wondered, strangely, if the falling snow-flakes kept a body warm in that high place. Other times she thought of a summer girl in a yellow dress dotted with red blossoms.

When her carer arrives in the room with a mug of tea, she will say, 'There's a bite in the mornings', and the older woman will ask 'Was I sleeping?' The steam will rise like incense from the mug and bubbles will congeal and burst on the liquid surface as she sips. She will rise and with her carer's help she will dress layer by layer; sitting for breath, rising again breathless; sitting, rising, dressing, layer by layer. She will pull the hair-net off her head and comb the fuzzy hair. She will pick silver hairs from the crimson comb.

After her carer leaves, perhaps she will shuffle down to the kitchen, open the dresser drawer and take out a tattered leather diary. She might select the year 1961 and read the staccato entries:

Ploughed March 20.
Sowed oats April 3.
Painted kitchen April 19 – magicote vinyl oyster.
Started cutting turf May 10.
Sold red heifer calf May 20.

She could re-live the slow progression of days and seasons that year, remind herself of the spring days as she sat and slit the seed potatoes, then pressed them into the crumbled soil, measuring the spaces between with her foot. A young girl measured out her smaller footprints on the sticky earth close to her.

The days moved to summer and the time came when red stubble-marks scraped the inside of her arms from tying sheaves of new-mown oats in August. All the time it seemed a girl walked close to her.

That year it was a golden September when Celia and her other children returned to school.

That year.

In the morning she walks in the kitchen with timid steps, inch by inch, panting breath by panting breath. She takes the novena book from the stool beside her chair and mouths the words:

Who is she that cometh forth as the morning rising,
fair as the moon, bright as the sun,
terrible as an army set in battle array?

She hears the bells toll at mid-day in the church of Saint Margaret Mary Alacoque. She nods off. If somebody looked through the window they would see her, mouth open, eyes closed but not tightly sealed, yellow dribble at the side of her mouth, wearing a skirt that is her second best.

When she sleeps in the afternoon it is of her own mother and her own childhood that she dreams: a woman with long hair tied back, holding the reins of a big grey stallion, lifting a child on to the horse; a woman who had helped the children ready the upturned sieve to catch the finches in the snow, and then lifted the sieve to release the captured birds once they had eaten the breadcrumbs. She is walking by the woman's side as she scatters crushed oats for the hens, and then gathers warm eggs from the straw into her apron pocket. She is being carried weightlessly by the woman, carried into the horizon by one who keeps her in safety.

She awakens and in that moment between waking and sleeping a strange memory comes to her – one that she had forgotten until somebody recently asked: 'What do you like to remember?'

She had replied that she liked to remember how they ran as children in the bogs at Gurteen, how they ran and jumped the bog-holes and laughed as they jumped from one side to the other. She held on to that memory – of running and laughing and skipping and jumping from this side, across the divide, to another place.

Months from now, a crowd will gather for the annual cemetery blessing high on the hill. The newly capped stonewall will separate them from the boggy fields and Knocknafola Hill. Those leaning on the wall will see a sole magpie flying low over rushes. As they look across to the oval lake at the bottom of the hill some will think of Sunday afternoons spent fishing for perch, when they gathered fat worms and tied lines and hooks to bamboo sticks. They will remember how their mothers fried fish for tea and warned them to watch for fish-bones.

The women will greet one another, admire fresh linen outfits and compare bronze tans and silver designer jewellery. Many decades have passed since they changed into summer clothes on the first day of May and clutched flowers to carry to the school to stuff in jam-jars for the May altar as they sang out:

Bring flowers of the fairest, bring flowers of the rarest
From garden and woodland and hillside and vale ...
O Mary we crown thee with blossoms today
Queen of the angels and Queen of the May.

The fingers of many of the May-day singers had been stained purple from pens dipped too eagerly into white ceramic ink-wells, ink that made frightful shapes on soft blotting-paper.

Several among them – those with good singing voices – had crossed the road many times and climbed the steps into the parish church of Saint Margaret Mary Alacoque. There the teacher pounded the groaning organ as they sang out:

Dies Irae, Dies Illa,
Solvet Saeclum In Favilla;
Teste David Cum Sibilla.

Then, on one unforgotten day, they sang out the words for one of their own.

While nobody mentions Celia she is in the minds of many as the priest splashes the children with holy water and intones:

May perpetual light shine upon them. May they rest in peace.

Several will look down to the ground, their minds filled with images – images of a yellow afternoon when the fruit of the horse-chestnut trees was beginning to fall and burst open showing snow-white insides; a morning when a group of children dared an auburn-haired girl to climb the high school wall that separated them from the long field beyond; then the sight of a body being tossed into the air.

Those who remember most clearly had been in the senior class with her. At the break, the senior girls had huddled together in the turf shed and opened lunches wrapped with loaf-paper. They spoke of leaving school, of boys, of dances, of daring. It was Celia, with her fiery hair, who took up the dare. Soon they were at the school wall urging her on, the boys in the adjacent school-yard joining in.

They will try hard to keep the memories at bay. The message sent from the school to Celia's mother in the pebble-dashed bungalow; the Doctor there before she arrived; the women trying to shield her from the gory sight. What did they think? Had she not faced the blood of birth when each of her children was born?

When prayers are finished the group will disperse and move around between headstones, pausing to chat and to pray. Some will avoid the place where the sun shines directly down and where a mound of fresh earth marks the spot of a recent internment, a spot where one body had been buried on top of another.

She opens the door into the front garden at dusk, moves outside and treads the grass softly, treads soil that has been beaten by generations of footprints. Her movements cause the blackbirds to take off in sudden darting flight like fistfuls of black confetti thrown into the air, drawing black patterns in the sky. She takes the birdseed and leaves it on the feeder table. It is an evening that she will turn her back on the red and lemon chinks of sunset in the sky above the place. Panting, breathless, she will move into the fading light of the room, footfalls ending at her high-backed chair. It is time.

A laughing freckle-face girl looks down from a picture on the shelf. She faces the woman whose mouth now hangs open, head to one side. A black cat prowls along the top of the wall beside the house. It stretches out its tail, its whiskers quivering in the grey light. It sniffs the dew-covered grass and throws itself claws first into the fuchsia hedge below and emerges with a small bird between its teeth. The bird skeleton is crunched like egg shells and its heart-beat ceases.

The tip of the moon disappears and a darkness envelopes the place. Not many days from now mother and daughter will share a space in that high place where magpies fly low over rushes. The ground will fold over itself and squeeze the air into its pockets. Mother and daughter will be folded together into the earth. In time, the bones of one will sink into those of the other. The sun will soon set over that place and rise again in the morning.

As it was in the beginning, is now and ever shall be.

Bust

by ALAN CADEN

The can of Dutch Gold goes through me almost as sharply as the wind. I have never had the bladder of an outside drinker. A thickening slow-motion mist of rain is descending, orange droplets visible in the streetlights, and it somehow finds its way in and around the bank's imposing stone porch. The rain in this city is heat-seeking, and I watch this strange race of people go by, heads sunken into their shoulders as if by evolution.

I must walk. This will relieve the pressure on my bladder, get my mind active. I have a diagnostic mind that regularly outpaces my will. I could have easily had a degree in medicine, you see. Just a year short of it. Then Amsterdam happened. Great times. Couldn't tell you exactly what happened there, but they were crazy times. Me and Manning have been in and out of Psych Ward ever since. Two, three … no, five years ago.

I scan the square. Martin is lolling on one of the stone benches, while Rosie endeavours to prop him up like some modern-day El Cid. A man in a nurse's uniform is doing push-ups while the replica of Pádraic Ó Conaire looks on disapprovingly. I feel empathy with the nurse – Pádraic always looks at me that way too. He has good reason, I suppose. I'd look like that too if I was only a replica and some students had knocked my head off and taken it back to Donegal with them. There! Walking up beside the tourist office, caught in the lights. What's his name? He was in school with me … David, probably. Worth a go. I position myself strategically at the exit point. I am Horatio on the bridge. He will not pass.

'Hiya David, how's it going? How's things? How are you? Still goin' out with yer wan that did the dirt on you? What's the craic? Long time, no? Where are you going tonight?'

Choose ONE question, David. In no more than 10 words,

describe your personal response.

He looks at me, his eyes a tangent of recognition, impatience and resignation. Pity would be nice. He keeps walking, on down Shop Street and I go with him. I'm losing him.

'Yeah yeah. Not so bad.' There is an awkward pause where one would normally ask 'and how are you?' but he can see that plainly. 'Eahh – I'm in a bit of a hurry.'

'Alright. Where are you going? You're limping a bit. What's up?'

'Just ... ah ... just down the town, to meet someone.'

My diagnosis of David: too honest to lie straight out. Isn't that admirable? Scent of deodorant, clean-shaven – meeting a woman. Doesn't want to feel like a mean bastard before he gets all romantic. Prospects are good.

'How's the business going? In your father's business now aren't you? Must get you to print me up some business cards – ha-ha, or a book. I have a great idea for a book. Any money?'

He hums, he haws, he keeps walking. So do I. End result, five euros – a good harvest. In the Other Skills section of my CV, if I had one, I should write, '*considerable experience in causing untenable levels of guilt in subjects*'. He was going to just give me small change, but it's hard when you know the person. I used to bully him in school too. I should feel sorry for that. I should feel a lot of things, but all I can feel is this fucking bladder. Bladder walls expanding, doctor, prognosis not good. What should we do? Seventy-five ml of Dutch Gold stat. Wait until he starts to go under. OK – let's bring him to the operating room. Let's extract this urine before he explodes. Nurse here, goddamit!

A line of taxis extend up the street, waiting for rain and closing time to pay their bills. I hold tightly onto my fiver. Three cans of cider at 5.4% each? No. Four Karpackie at 4.8% works out better. Drinking has helped me learn Polish. Four. That way, if those girls turn up again I can offer them a can. I'd shag them senseless if it wasn't for these fucking drugs. They keep me level, though. Level. I reach into my coat pocket and shake the plastic pill bottle. No sound. Tomorrow is … Thursday? Got to go down to the Ward so.

There are too many people around for me to answer the call of the wild, to mark my territory. I'll go to the offie after I dispose of the evening's beverages. Across the road is a pub, The Living Room. I don't need Lebensraum, I need Pissing Room, and a little warmth too, so it's worth a try. I ghost up to the doorway and am confronted with a bouncer. Large, simian, blonde shaven head. Bomber jacket. Diagnosis: Polish. I don't know whether to say something to him or not. He doesn't know whether to stop me or not. I don't look too bad today – I was up home at the weekend and got new clothes, a shave, good food. A mother's tears. What bottomless well do those tears come from? 'Cos mine are long gone.

'Karpackie', I say, and nod confidently at him. He doesn't step out of my way. He doesn't stop me either.

Where's the fucking jacks in this place? It's packed. Thumping music. The kind the girls like and the lads tolerate because the girls like it. A heaving mass of lurid colours and people pretending to be normal. Minimalist shite filled with maximalist arseholes. I want to pick up a giant glass and smash it over all their heads. Again and again. Hold on, doctor – bladder critical. Symptoms include murderous fantasies, extreme impatience. We need to operate, now!

I slip through the crowd. My ears are pounding. I'm roasting but my Dutch Gold is precariously balanced in the inside pocket of my duffel coat. It's good and warm. My mother gave it to me at the weekend. Used to belong to my brother. He doesn't talk to me anymore, but who's wearing the jacket now, bro!

Are all these people thinking thoughts while they talk? Are they hating, loving, lusting, filthy behind their smiling faces?

'Watch it, ya tool!'

He's a big man. Pink polo shirt, designer unkempt hair with highlights, bright red mammy-pinched cheeks. Diagnosis: wanker. He backed into me, in the middle of animated motions to describe a story of which he is the comical hero. I do not apologise. I do not aggravate. I stop and look at him. His friends gape at him, expectantly. He's the funny guy, but he's also the violent guy (they've all heard the stories but never seen him fight). He takes a drink of his ... sniff sniff ... vodka and Red Bull and winds up for a hilarious put-down.

'Where's the bathroom, man?' my bladder forces me to ask before he can unleash his wit. Confused, he points over to the blue-lit outline of a stick-man. I am gone before his quick tongue can unleash a challenge. Priorities. I'd love to duel but I can't hold out much longer.

The zip of my jeans is rusted and hard to open. I can feel the piss rising, longing to return to the sea. To the sea. Lonely rivers flow to the sea. There is a black in the jacks, purveying a variety of guilt-marketed smellies. I nod at him while I fumble with my zip. When I get this organ-warmed Dutch Gold decanted I'll ask him where he's from. I catch a blur of pink, an increase in noise before the door swings closed and he's there beside me. Wankstain himself.

I break the zip but get it open and manoeuvre my already dripping lad into position. Oh sweet relief. The madness of life when all of your satisfaction is distilled into one excretory function. Beside me, Tight-head Prop is doing the same, with his free hand leaning against the fake-Arabic tiles in that old-man style you see in Guinness pubs.

'Hey, the littlest Hobo, what the fuck are you looking at?'

Choice of responses: a) 'not much', b) 'don't know – don't have a microscope', c) 'a drunk girl's disappointment', or d) 'sorry, man – sometimes I stare too long at people, it's the drugs, I think.'

I choose none of the above and instead keep staring. This will annoy him even more.

'Faggot.'

We are both still pissing. He is Angel Falls (a higher free-fall), but I am Iguazú (greater volume). He returns his glare intently down to the trough of the urinal. What is he looking at? In the trough there is one cube of hard soap of a radioactive yellow colour. His stream is pushing it toward my direction. He's doing this on purpose, the bastard! I must stop him. I direct my own steaming flow onto the edge of the cube and turn it. For a moment, the cube wavers, dances on a corner beneath the combined pressure until I squeeze all the might of my bladder muscles and loosen my sphincter. He cannot withstand the power of my bladder, despite his greatest efforts, and the cube spins inexorably towards his end of the urinal and victory. I am the Urinolympics champion! An open-top bus through the streets of the city, please. Next time I hope to compete in the High Piss, the Long Piss and the Hop, Skip and Piss. I keep the pressure on, continue my stream in an arc to make sure, but I am a little over-eager and I splash all over his slip-on shoes and stone-washed jeans (didn't they go out with the 80s?). I feel embarrassed that the poor black fella has to clear up my mess, but must first finish off. A sprinter cannot stop dead simply because he has crossed the line. I stop, start again, stop, then shake out the last few drops to rapturous applause.

Then he smashes my head against the tiles with enough force that I hear something crack (my zygomatic bone? the tiles?). I crumple in a heap, face down in the cooling remnants of my triumph, and he kicks me once in the neck and once in the sternum before the black man, who is bigger than either of us, pulls him off. Before I know what has happened I am outside on the street, attracting onlookers as a bouncer holds me up. He feels obliged to ask me (once) if I am okay, then props me against a wall and tells me not to come back. Pinkie is nowhere to be seen.

Dizziness, confusion, and a general sense of elation. Diagnosis: mild concussion.

Later on, it must be about four because most of the night-club crowd have wandered off home, I am on my last can up in Eyre Square. Didn't see those girls around. I swapped one of my cans with Martin for a few slugs of his Irish Cream while I regaled him with the story. Pricks like that always get the benefit of the doubt. I don't think my cheek-bone is broken but my teeth are beginning to hurt. I try to get the cold liquid down my throat without it touching them but it's not easy. I huddle in the doorway and imagine being him. An arsehole. Normal, successful and confident. But I don't want to be him. And I ask myself why not. I ask Eyre Square.

The Method

by PATRICIA BYRNE

Murder can be daunting if, like me, you've no experience. The Internet is a great help nowadays, an easy way to find a hired hit. It's efficient and takes you out of the loop. You do your planning and execute through an easy 1-2-3 order process. It's clean.

You're obsessed with the small, blond-haired man in the pink shirt. Does he always wear a pink shirt or is it that the image that has got into your mind like a brain-worm? His every move, his every feature is etched into your brain. He was the one who should have taken away your fragility.

You need to get the planning right. Step 1 – select *Target* from the web menu options. That's easy. You're surprised at the extent of the targets list: 20 of them, starting with *Husband* and ending with *Yourself*, with *Boss* in the middle. *Boss* – that's your target. The small man in the pink shirt.

You're all in the long meeting room, around an oval oak table. He's seated at one end, jacket thrown casually over his shoulders, at the ready. You sit opposite him, smile at him, think of how little he knows of what's going on in your head. He has everything ready: his file of meeting papers neat on his right, the secretary sitting up close on his left. He drums his fingers on the table, looks at his watch and waits for people to arrive. All the time your brain is working on the plan. For him, the hours, the days and nights you shared are long forgotten, as if they never happened.

Step 2 – select your termination method. Here it gets serious. *Shooting* is the 'timeless classic'. The weapon choices are small-calibre handgun, shotgun or high-powered rifle. *Stabbing* is painful but gives the target time to think about things before their life comes to an unpleasant end. *Strangling* is suitable for females and small or weak males:

its advantage is that it doesn't involve blood-letting. Spilt blood terrifies you and has done for as long as you remember. *Burning* has no appeal – not keen on incendiary options at all. You scroll to the *NEW* option that's just been added to the menu. It's *MELTING* and involves 'total body immersion in hydrofluoric acid'. The body is totally liquefied and results in the target becoming the subject of a missing person case. Neat.

He has written comments on the papers in front of him. The writing is small, neat, controlled, wormy: *Where is the auditor's cert? Should we not get legal opinion? Is there compliance with the guidelines? Are these conditions standard?* You are mesmerised by the small, tight handwriting of the man in the pink shirt; driven to distraction you are. You wait for things to hot up, for his knuckles to go white, for the rage to build, for the finger-tapping on the table to quicken, the drumming of small, neat, manicured fingers. The tension builds in your head. You're thinking of the options – the extermination options. You're thinking about the 'classic method'. You want it to be neat and quick.

You first saw a gun up close in a cafe off Barcelona's Place de Catalonia. That day had started out well but would dip and rise like the waves and curves of the facades of the buildings of the 'hallucinogenic Gaudi', Barcelona's favourite son. His Casa Battlo brimmed with blues, mauves and greens, with images of octopus and star-fish. It reminded you of the house with wobbly windows in the Hansel and Gretel story. That pair knew all about incendiary terminations. Straight lines were not Gaudi's thing at all. No, the man was into curves and arcs and soaring shapes inspired by his native Tarragona. Poor Antoni met his end when run over by a train in central Barcelona in 1926. Was it accidental? Was he pushed? When they found him, all he carried was a handful of currants and peanuts in his coat pocket.

What will the small man in the pink shirt have in his pocket when they find him?

You ate in a tapas bar off the Place de Catalonia. You ate fried anchovies, goat's cheese and salad. You drank a large glass of cava. The bar was packed. You put your bag on the ground close to your feet. You drank too much cava. The crowd jostled and pushed. Then, there was a man beside you showing a police identification card. He held up your bag in his other hand. He gestured towards the door where his colleague pointed a gun at the culprit. The police had pursued him. He was caught in the act. It was the first real gun you saw. It looked elegant. You were glad there was no shooting. You don't like the look of blood.

Next day you visited Gaudi's unfinished cathedral, the Sagrada Familia. You were in need of purification. You raised your head to the giant spires that looked like they were licking heaven. It's said that Gaudi was inspired by the mountain peaks of Montserrat – the holy mountain. You raised your head to the tangled sculpture masses of Catalonian fruit and plants. You had no thoughts of guns or blood or termination options.

That day you were pure.

Nowadays you are different, fascinated by termination methods. Take the growth of copycat killings – like the two school massacres in Finland. It seems that the two incidents may have been connected; the two killers may have been in contact. They bought their guns in the same city. The locals cannot believe this could happen in their sleepy town. They think it's a dream. They lay flowers under a Finnish flag flying at half-mast. Matti was a happy normal guy – nothing special about him. He was quiet, almost invisible you could say.

But Matti Saari hated the human race. He left notes saying that he hated, that he was motivated by hate. He went on a 90-minute shooting spree. He wore black, dressed in a ski mask. He was a man obsessed – obsessed with guns, obsessed with hate.

He used a .22 calibre Walther automatic pistol. He can be seen firing shots on a posted *YouTube* video. Alongside the clip he posted a message: *Whole life is war and whole life is pain.* How could this happen in a sleepy town in western Finland? How could this place harbour such a disturbed mind?

Guns were his hobby, guns and computers and sex and beer. He was a silent young man, his school principal said. He was a young man with two faces.

He telephoned a friend during the shooting. He told him he had just shot ten people. He was calling to say goodbye; he was going to kill himself; he wanted to be cremated. After he shot them he set fire to the classroom. He wanted to burn all the bodies beyond recognition. He hated everything about the human race.

Not you, you don't hate the human race. You're not into hatred. You just want one person removed from the face of the earth, the person who could have guaranteed your happiness, made your life whole.

You have difficulty settling on a preferred method. *Drugging* can be clean and discreet and has the advantage that it could appear as an overdose of recreational or prescription drugs. In *Accidental* the hitman covertly follows the target, gets to know their habitual behaviour and carefully plans an 'accident'. All is discreet. It will seem that the unfortunate target was the victim of a tragic accident. Much less discreet is *Plummeting*, which is designed to attract a lot of attention. The target is thrown from the maximum possible height. No injuries are inflicted before the fall, so foul play is not suspected. Too much choice for a novice. You've definitely ruled out *Bludgeoning* – far too gruesome.

The man in pink is talking with controlled rage. You know what he's saying without really listening. He's repeating himself: *The standard of documentation is not acceptable. I hold you responsible. I need to have the files well in advance; timely circulation; time to examine the facts of each case. I need this. I insist. How many times have I to say it? Are you listening?* You never stop listening. You never get his voice out of your head.

Your left hand is in a plaster, after you sliced your finger on sharp glass. Sliced it right through and almost took off the bone. The blood splashed all over the room. You couldn't understand how there could be so much blood. You stood there wondering if you should clean the room or try to stop the finger bleeding. You had to wrap the bandage round and round until the blood stopped seeping through. They removed the bandage at the hospital Accident & Emergency. They told you to leave your hand on a metal table. They let it bleed and bleed until you thought there was no more blood left.

It's four decades since a gun-man took out John F. Kennedy. You were a rookie boarder, an innocent, when he was shot. It was just weeks after your mother said her goodbyes in the parlour of the convent school. There was a smell of polish everywhere; the dark wood and golden brasses gleamed. She didn't cry when she left. You have often wondered if she cried on the way home.

You woke up that first morning in a dormitory cubicle with white calico curtains pulled all round. The white, stainless calico was crisp with starch. You were beginning to settle in when the shooting happened. You heard the news in the evening time, seated in a study hall of long desk lines. President Kennedy has been shot in Dallas. President Kennedy is dead.

Your mother posted all the newspapers to the school. You saw a woman trying to crawl from the back of the open-top limousine. She tried to crawl on all fours from the blood; she tried to get away. She wouldn't take the suit off. You could see the stains on the pink suit when she stood beside Lyndon Johnson for his swearing-in. Governor John Connolly and his wife Nellie were in the motorcade. Nellie talked afterwards about the roses being spattered with blood. According to one version of events, the gun-man pointed his gun from a window high up. He got his aim spot-on.

They got Martin Luther King that spring on a balcony of the Lorraine Hotel in Memphis, Tennessee after he spoke the words: *And I've seen the Promised Land ... I'm not fearing any man ... Mine eyes have seen the glory of the coming of the Lord.*

The bullet entered his jaw.

You were sitting in the school hall watching a science programme when you heard about Robert Kennedy. The class was spending its last days and weeks together before heading into the big bad world. One of the bullets went through his ear. They cradled his head. His children grew up watching video images of his shooting being played over and over. The Kennedy shootings sandwiched your years of growing, your years of innocence.

Blood stains on pink roses.

Stainless white calico.

Bullets ripping through heads.

Johnny Cash singing *Ring of Fire.*

The pink man is talking. *I want all documentation a week in advance of the meeting. Do you hear what I'm saying?* He taps the table and glares across at you. He knows nothing about your bleeding finger and your blood splattered all over the room. He knows nothing about the gun. He knows nothing about what goes on in your head. He straightens his tie, lifts his shoulders and arranges his papers. He is ready. *Minutes of last Meeting. Matters Arising.* You look at him. He looks at you. He lacks imagination. He has no idea, this small blonde man in the pink shirt. He knows nothing about your two faces. He has no idea.

Step 3 – time to choose, to execute the plan. They kept the intriguing methods until last. The *Works* package is one of the best sellers and combines several options in an 'overkill, which makes a radical statement'. The *Surprise* package is for the adventurous client and allows the hit man to select the termination method based on his mood at a particular time. If you're the nervous type, this method allows you to plead genuine innocence of what might have happened.

You're veering towards *Apparent Suicide* – a good option in quiet locations where murders would draw too much attention. There are different approaches here: a single gun-shot would make it appear that the shot came from the target's own hand; or poisoning – now there's a real possibility.

One way or another, you'll settle for something that's not excessively violent. You're not into violence.

An Unkindness of Ravens, A Murder of Crows

by MÁIRE T. ROBINSON

Once Declan made the decision, he found it easy to become a bird-watcher. It wasn't like golf where you had to learn the rules, join a club, and wear diamond-patterned socks. He simply bought a pair of binoculars, a notebook, a pen, and a copy of *Bird-Watching in Ireland*. He could amble along now, alone, but with a sense of purpose. Not happy exactly, but occupied.

Ross's Gull (*Rhodostethia rosea*)
Named after the North Pole explorer, James Clark Ross, it is the only species in its genus. Identification:

Small pale grey and white gull with wedge-shaped tail and distinctive black collar around the neck

Deep pink hue on breast during breeding season

Similar in size and plumage to the Little Gull (*Hyrocoloeus minutus*) but larger and longer winged (See picture overleaf)

When Declan was six, he found an injured bird cowering in the corner of the garden. At the time he thought it was a blackbird, but looking back on it now, it was probably a baby rook. It had been attacked by something, the neighbours' fat tomcat most likely. The bird beat its wings pathetically, but could not fly. It emitted startled squawks. Declan scooped it up carefully in an empty cardboard box and brought it into the kitchen. His father looked at it and shook his head. He took the tiny creature up into his hands.

'For its own good,' he said to Declan. He placed his fingers around the bird's neck. And there was a sharp snapping sound, like a dry twig.

It was incredible, the variety of birds you could see in Galway City, once you knew what you were looking for. There were grey wagtails and dipper in the Corrib and in the canals. There were herons and kingfisher in Lough Atalia. In late April and early May you could see whimbrel on Mutton Island, enjoying their annual trip to the sewage treatment plant. The best time of all, though, was winter.

Declan no longer dreaded winter. It no longer meant Christmas day alone and Helen's annual call, her voice full of pity and contempt. His son being put on the phone and told to 'thank daddy' for this year's unwanted present. Now, winter meant standing on Nimmo's Pier spotting the gulls. Not just any old gulls. Rare gulls. Special gulls that birdwatchers from all over the world flocked to see.

NIMMO'S PIER, Jan 8:
3 x American Herring gull
4 x Ring-billed gull

Declan closed his notebook and put it and his pen back into the inside pocket of his Parka. No Ross's Gull. He would have to come back tomorrow. There had been reports of sightings on birdwatchers' websites a couple of days ago. It was starting to rain. He pulled his gloves back on and started to walk up the Pier, towards town. There was a lone dark-haired woman taking shelter under the Spanish Arch. She was wearing a crimson woolly hat and Declan noticed the binoculars around her neck. As he approached her, she suddenly waved at him and beamed widely. There was a general camaraderie between bird-watchers. Recognition of their common pursuit was usually acknowledged with a smile or a nod. The woman's familiarity with him made him stall. Did she know him? An old friend of Helen's maybe? But then, surely, she wouldn't be waving at him so cheerily.

'Here to see the gulls?' she called and he realised he didn't know her at all. She was just one of those people. She probably talked to strangers on trains.

Rook (*Corvus frugilegus*)

Identification:

A species of crow with all black plumage, which can show a red or purple sheen in certain light

Intelligent and social in nature

Similar in appearance to the carrion crow, but the rook has a more peeked crown

She asked him if he knew of a good spot for a bite to eat. 'Nothing fancy.' He knew just the place. He led her in the opposite direction from the Italian restaurants and eateries of Quay Street, like two salmon swimming upstream.

She offered him her hand to shake. 'I'm Gladys.'

'Declan.'

Her hand was as fragile and white as one of Helen's china cups.

They crossed Wolf Tone Bridge and went to a place he knew on Dominick Street. Gladys smiled when she saw the linoleum floor, the faded floral PVC tablecloths, and the framed photograph of the Pope's visit to Ireland.

After Helen left him, he had come here a lot. You got a decent feed and didn't have to pay an arm and a leg. Helen used to laugh and say he only thought he'd eaten a proper dinner if it included potatoes. She tried to make him eat pasta and cous cous. At least he could eat whatever he wanted now. There was always a silver lining.

He looked at Gladys sitting opposite him. She had removed her heavy duffel coat and looked tiny, perched on her seat. She was wearing a black woollen jumper, a black skirt to the knee, and thick black tights. She had on those furry boots women seemed to favour these days. She took off her rain-soaked red hat. The fluorescent light shone on Gladys from overhead, making her hair glint with iridescent streaks of purple, like Indian ink. He wondered if she dyed it. His own hair had started turning grey when he was twenty-one. He decided she was definitely younger than him, but not by much. If he had to guess, he'd say she was thirty-five. If she asked him to guess, he'd say thirty. He rubbed his hand over his chin and thought to himself that he really must shave. He could feel the prickles of hair on his neck sticking into his black polo neck.

Gladys ordered the stew with a side portion of brown bread. Declan ordered the roast turkey dinner, with potatoes. He smiled at Gladys. 'For someone so small you've a big appetite.' Then he worried it was the wrong thing to say. Women could be funny about food, he knew that much, but she beamed widely.

'I'm starving! I've been standing on that pier all day.'

Her voice didn't sound like it belonged to her. She looked like she should have the high-pitched voice of a tiny girl. It was a deep conspiratorial voice. Every sentence sounded like she was letting him in on a secret, just between the two of them.

It would be rude not to invite her for a drink, thought Declan. She was from Wicklow and didn't know anyone in town. Otherwise she'd just be sitting there, bored, in her B&B on College Road. He brought her to *Freeney's* and they sat in the corner. The pub hadn't changed in donkeys' years and there was something reassuring about that. There must be a recommendation for it in some tourist book or other, something about 'the genuine Irish pub experience'. He often spotted rain-coated tourists surveying the bar and sipping Guinness tentatively. She asked for a white wine, which he felt showed a touch of class. Helen drank vodka, but then Helen drank anything. That was the problem, at least as he saw it.

Gladys told him she'd grown up near Kilcoole, where her father had taken her bird-watching at weekends. She'd learnt early on to recognise the different species: lapwing, brent, curlew. When most little girls were asking for teddy bears and Barbie dolls for their birthdays, Gladys was asking for binoculars and bird books. Declan thought of Sean, how he'd envisioned buying him his own pair of binoculars. In the early days he'd had big plans for Sean's monthly visits. These days there was always some excuse: a friend's birthday, a football match. When he did come to stay, he moved about Declan's house like a ghost. He spent his time playing computer games or cocooned by giant headphones.

Declan felt a lump in his throat. He coughed.

'Same again?' asked Gladys.

She asked him if he'd heard about the ravens in Britain. He shook his head as he took a long swig of his pint.

'There's been reports of flocks attacking livestock,' she said. 'The farmers want their protected status lifted, so they can shoot them.'

'That can't be right. It's carrion they eat, unless the animals were sick, or dying.'

'No, the farmers said the animals were healthy. The ravens ate them alive. Pecked out their eyes. Ate their tongues and their underbellies.'

As the lights flashed for last orders they were taking turns, listing group names for birds. It had started as a way to fill a lull in the conversation.

He presented her with 'A bouquet of pheasants.'

She accepted with 'A charm of finches.'

He offered her 'A murmuration of starlings.'

She gave him 'A tidings of magpies.'

When he opened the door to his house, and she followed him inside, he saw it through her eyes and immediately knew he'd made a mistake in inviting her. He inhaled the musty dank smell of the place. He removed the pile of newspapers from the chair in the sitting room and gestured for her to sit down. There was a cold clamminess to the air that stuck to skin like wet clothing. He saw the dirty cups and plates on the table, the take-away curry that had solidified in its container.

'Sorry the place is such a mess.'

'Oh, mine is much worse,' she laughed, 'believe me.'

He didn't believe her.

As they drank tea, Declan could feel the ease of the night slipping away, like sand from his hands. Gladys sat with her coat and hat still on. He couldn't read her. What was he supposed to say, do? Was he supposed to sit here and talk about birds all night? What did she want?

Gladys looked at her watch.

'I should be getting back to the B&B. It's getting late.'

'Right, ok, well, I'll walk you.'

'No, honestly, it's ok,' she said, standing up, 'thanks for the tea.'

Declan knew it was too late. Ruined.

'Well, I'll probably see you at ...'

She stopped. 'Are you ok?'

He wiped his eyes. 'I'm fine, I'm fine.'

'Are you sure you ...'

'I said I'm fine, honestly.'

He bit his lip. Couldn't look her in the eye. Stared at his shoes, willing her to disappear.

'Declan, is there ...'

He felt her hand on his arm. The pitying touch. Jesus to a leper.

'Just go,' he said.

'I don't understand, was it something I ...'

'Get out! Just get the fuck out!'

He tried to get the words out, to apologise, to explain to her. She was backing away, her face pale. If he could just explain. If he could stop crying. Something in her face, the trace of a sneer, reminded him of Helen. He could taste rage and shame in his throat. He only reached out his hands to grab her by the shoulders to calm her, to make her see. He saw his hands encircling her slender neck. And there was a sharp snapping sound.

Jan 9:

They are everywhere. If you listen you will hear them, over the noise of the workman's drilling, the school children's bullying, the boy racers' beeping. They wail like newborns, scream like vengeful spirits. They swim with the shit and the beer cans in the canal. They roost on rooftops, scavenge our rubbish, eat our scraps. They live beside us and above us. They watch us, and sometimes we look back.

Lonely Hearts Club

by DARA Ó FOGHLÚ

This is my seventh blind date in as many weeks. I come back from the bar with two glasses of red wine and we sit facing each other at a small table in the corner of a pub. She says her name is Sheryl but she could be lying. Dark eyebrows and muddy hair down to her shoulder blades. In her profile photo she was blonde. *Blonde*. We clink glasses. She smiles. I smile. Her fingers fidget autonomously, peeling shreds of paper off a beer mat. I should have had a drink to loosen up before meeting her. I almost say, 'I really like this place, don't you?' But I don't. I've said that already. So the silence snowballs, drowning out the band's sound check in the next room.

'Check. Chew – chew. One – chew.'

Liars can't bear gaps in conversation. So she starts telling me about palmistry and how the spaces between fingers indicate an open personality.

'Show me your hand,' she says.

Her speech is already slurred. The gaps between my fingers are supposed to mean I'm an honest person.

'Thass good,' she says.

She must have stopped for a drink somewhere before meeting me. Before I can think of something better to talk about, Sheryl suggests we tell each other a secret so we won't be strangers any more. I'm pretty sure she stole that from a movie.

'We can say anything?'

'Anything. We have total amnesty.'

There's no such thing as total amnesty. Everyone gets judged by what they say. That's the reason people lie. 'Okay,' I say. 'Ladies first.'

'Right,' she says, burping silently into her tiny fist. 'There's an old woman on my street who used to be my primary school teacher. You don't really need to know her real name. A class of hers from the seventies called her Swamp Thing and it stuck. When I was five, I wet myself in her class because she wouldn't let me go to the toilet. She pointed out the puddle under my seat and made me stand at the blackboard with everyone watching drips from my school dress fall into my shoes. My socks squelched all the way home and I was called pissy-pants until mum moved me to a new school.'

'Hey, if it makes you feel any better I pissed myself in primary school too.' I hadn't, but women like it when you have things in common with them.

'That wasn't the secret bit.'

'Oh.'

'Anyway, so now Swamp Thing lives on my street. Alone. She never married and, as far as I can tell, she has no friends. So I just …'

'… What?'

'I just mess with her a bit.'

'Go on.'

'It's all petty stuff really, but I've kept it up for over a year now. I get pizzas delivered to her house; taxis. Sometimes I'll ring her doorbell and run off. And every now and then, when I know she's gone shopping, I'll sneak in through her back window and take a piss in her chest of drawers.'

'Seriously?'

'Oh yeah. She thought that just 'cos I was a kid I couldn't do anything about it. But I can now. I can do it all over her stupid flowery dresses.' She drained her glass of wine and sat back in her chair. 'God. I feel better already. Now, your turn and don't hold out on me.'

I'm not sure exactly which way to lie. Does she want to hear me say I beat my ex-girlfriend? Should I tell her I was in jail or something? If I admit that I just don't want to be alone any more and I'm willing to do anything for some human contact, will she run away like the others?

I watch porn all the time. I didn't tell Sheryl that though. I don't really like much of it, and it's a poor substitute for a girlfriend. The endings are always unsurprising, and there's an awful lot of spitting on one another and hair pulling – 'take it you bitch,' and so on. These people never stop and smile at each other. It seems like they are always avoiding eye contact – I suppose they're a bit embarrassed, thinking about what their parents might say.

The world would be a kinder place if porn was just two people having a hug, if they said, 'I love you,' and 'I love you too.' But you can't get that on any of these porn sites. Instead they have 'Teen slut drilled by two guys'; 'Anime girl raped by tentacles'; 'Carla gets pissed on and cries'. You get used to anything after a while.

There is a three-minute video clip aptly captioned 'Gwen gets banged' where a Rubenesque Gwen does her best to look and sound interested while a man, who probably isn't her significant other, thrashes away at her business end. He has been on a sunbed but left his y-fronts on, so it looks like he is wearing seamless white underpants. He looks to poor plain Gwen and says, 'Are you ready for my cock, baby?'

And she turns to the camera and says with tragic earnestness, 'Yes, I am.' Her expression is forced, like she'd rather be somewhere else, doing something else.

'Look at the camera,' he tells her.

And she does. I really wish she wouldn't. She stares it down, her chubby face framed by a bob of purple-dyed hair and her bad tattoos jiggling in the tide of their motion.

'Oh yeah,' she says.

'Oh baby,' he says.

They are on a grey bedspread laid out on a grey carpet. A hi-fi speaker sits in the corner of the camera shot but there's no music playing. Gwen looks distinctly unenthused and self-conscious as her red-faced lover charges and retreats. Poor Gwen. Poor fat Gwen. Her pedestrian performance earned her 3.6 stars out of 5 and was judged by 255,898 people. I made it 255,899. Poor fat, ugly, lonely Gwen – captured at her most vulnerable, her flabby boobs dancing on her bulging midriff, the crease of her belly like a sunless valley crushed between two drumlins. I think this is about as far away from love as you can get. I miss being in love, and I bet Gwen does too. I'd like to give her a hug, maybe tell her to put some clothes on and I'd make her a nice salad.

It was next to Gwen's clip that I saw the ad for the dating agency. It said, 'Click. Date. Marry.' These sites are honey-traps for career nerds and the terminally introverted, all of us frantically sifting through the bargain bin of women past their use-by date, salvaging or dismissing them based on their dimensions, hobbies, or what their favourite meal is.

I used to have a girlfriend. Bethan. She was a natural blonde and had soft-focus features lifted straight from a celebrity magazine – nothing like Gwen. On our first date I brought her to the cinema to see a film – a real tear-jerker. When the little girl in the movie found her crippled father overdosed on painkillers, Bethan just laughed with her mouth full of popcorn. Couples behind us sent up a chorus of 'tut-tuts' and practiced sighs, but she kept on giggling and snorting until she was done. She had a talent for finding the joke in every tragedy.

When we started dating, the sex was all about galvanising our trust – translating the things there were no words for. Then one night in her flat, she asked me if I wanted to watch a movie.

'I love movies,' I said.

Suffice it to say, it was no *Casablanca*. After that, she started introducing other things into the bedroom: root vegetables, cuffs, clothes-pegs, fighting. She liked that whole rough-and-tumble version of sex and I played along because I wanted to make her happy. You do that when you're in love. No relationship ever works without compromise, but on the day you wake up wearing a dog-collar and can't sit down without hurting you know you've lost sight of who you used to be. That's not compromise. That's domination. You are Poland.

She is Nazi Germany. Then one day she's gone and you can't remember how a normal relationship is supposed to work.

Nowadays love letters and hand-in-hand strolls along the beach have been outdone by facials, pearl necklaces and golden showers. Lovemaking is either a community sport where anyone can join in, or an individual endurance test where you try and beat your personal best. It is a competition where nobody is winning. Not Gwen and certainly not me. I'm spending my thirties in the shopping queue for damaged goods surrounded by the legion of socially inept.

Sheryl was one of the better ones, really. There were others.

Karen's profile says she likes movies that don't scare her and her favourite actor is 'Phoebe from *Friends*'. She works at a perfume counter in the city centre and the reason she doesn't have a boyfriend is because men have always been intimidated by her stunning beauty. 'Stunning beauty.' Her words.

Above the list of her likes and dislikes, including her least favourite colour (mustard) is a smiling headshot of Karen. Her hair is a thick cloud of tight red curls like a million rusted bedsprings wired into her skull. She is so pebble-dashed with freckles that we could spend the rest of our lives together, rocking our chairs on the front porch and playing join-the-dots on her face. Her lips are busy wringing out a smile that tries to convince the world that yes, she is having a good time, but her eyes admit that she is a long way off fooling herself.

I clicked the next profile.

My name is Melody. I'm a Scorpio (not interested in Geminis or Capricorns). This is a terrible photo of me. I'm much prettier in real life. Click. *I'm Annette. I'm looking for someone who won't lie to me. Someone who is interested in art, literature and classical music. No Jews.* Click. *You can call me Mother Superior. Pray with me, sinner.* Click.

It went on like this for some time before I found Sheryl. She wears the same perfume as Bethan. That's good. If any of what she put in her profile is true, I know that she likes to walk the shoreline on stormy nights. She goes barefoot in summertime and she likes strong men. I think that means she likes bastards. That's where I've been going wrong. I have arrived with flowers or chocolates for my last six dates. I opened doors for them and complimented them on their plain faces. Women don't want that. They want a challenge. They want a bastard to tame. That's why Bethan left me. She had nothing left to change.

'So ...' Sheryl says, 'you owe me one embarrassing secret.'

'Sorry, I can't think of anything.'

The Messenger

by COLM BRADY

Mick got off the bus followed by Gubmund. They turned and walked through wrought iron gates and onto a tree-lined avenue leading to the school buildings.

'Did you see that Spitting Image on last night?'

'No, was it on RTÉ?'

'Oh I forgot ye haven't got into the 1980s yet. Would ye not put up an aerial like everyone else?'

'It's the transmitter up the road.'

'Oh yeah, the transmitter.'

'We can get RTÉ even when the coat-hanger falls out but nothing else. One of the neighbours put up a thirty foot aerial then it collapsed and killed his dog. The ould fellah says we should learn from his mistakes.'

'But you don't have a dog.'

'I didn't bother mentioning that.'

Mick glared at the tarmac as they crossed the threshold of the grounds proper.

'What the fuck are you wearing on your feet?'

'They got them at the weekend. The ould lass says they're loafers.'

'But they're brown, and they have heels.'

'They're tan and that's what loafers look like.'

'One of them is tan and the other one is dark tan. Where did they get them?'

'They just sort of appeared. I thought they might have got them on the markets in the North. Are they that bad?'

'If anyone sees them you're fuckin' dead. What colour are everyone else's shoes?'

Gubmund glanced around and looked deflated. 'They're grey and a few black pairs. I'm in trouble, amn't I?'

'They'll eat you alive. If the boarders spot them, you don't want to know what they will do. Remember when Lambo came in all proud of the duffel coat that his Mammy bought him?'

'Yeah Fucus and the boarders brought it into the urinals and ... Jesus, me shoes! I can't go home wearing a pair of piss containers!'

'I'm afraid it's worse than that, captain. I don't reckon those heels belong on a pair of men's shoes. I think you are swanning into this kip in a pair of brown women's shoes that don't match. The only reason they will piss on them is if they set them on fire first.'

'You know the smokies called at our house in a Hiace on Saturday; you don't think the shoes came from them do you? That would be instant death in this place. They hate poor people but they hate smokies even more.'

'That's cos the smokies don't give a fuck about them and would beat seven colours of shite out of them given any excuse.'

'Jesus, women's shoes; this is gonna get nasty. Yer man Ethics got declared bent just for saying that word in English.'

'What word?'

'"Ethics." He only said it once. He doesn't seem to mind being a bender but I'm fucked if – '

'You will be if the boarders get you. You need protection, someone hard. Someone like Mongo.'

'What have I got that that lunatic needs? He hits priests for fuck sake! He doesn't give a shite about a couple of farmers with no money.'

'Well, I hear his last messenger is suspended. Mongo is doing a nice trade in selling loose Rothmans, chocolate and other stuff for the boarders. If we take a detour by the smoking shed we might just catch him.'

Smoking was prohibited in the whole school with one exception. Students who had permission from their parents could use a shelter beside the soccer pitches. With the literal-mindedness that all adolescent boys possess it became known as 'the smoking shed'. It was understood that no priest was going to raid the shed seeking parental notes and Mongo was there to ensure there was no glue-sniffing or homosexuality on the premises.

The etiquette was that when a cigarette was lit up, boys would clamour for first drag. In a base three system, as complicated as anything the Babylonians came up with, a drag consisted of three pulls. A pull in turn consisted of three blasts, which was the lowest graduation of nicotine available. Mongo was the exception to this convention: he just took whatever he wanted.

He was surprised to see the two farmers stick their heads into the shed. He was deep in conversation with his deputy, a gangly boarder known universally as 'Fucus' on a matter of some import. A fourth year had the temerity to strike back at a Leaving Cert. bully and by all accounts had given the guy a fairly comprehensive beating. The Leaving Certs. wanted to put manners on the junior year who in turn wanted to end years of oppression. If they went down the brawling route there would be a discipline issue for the priests and people would get suspended. More importantly, the petty scams that Mongo ran would be disrupted by a war. He and Fucus quickly decided that a prizefight between the two parties would be arranged for the following Wednesday.

Mick and Gubmund walked over to his bench as Mongo lit a cigarette.

'Smoke, gentlemen?' Gubmund had recently got over the bouts of nausea and dizziness that cigarettes caused but had yet to get to the stage where he actually enjoyed them.

'I'll take first drag.'

Fucus wandered off to accost some younger boarders, glancing at the ground looking for butts. As he passed Gubmund, he stopped to get another look.

'Nice shoes, man.'

Once the sentence hit the cold concrete it shattered and spread. People were in shock that anyone would have the gall to sport such footwear in the shed. Mongo liked to think he was broad-minded; he despised everyone equally and if they decided one day to wear two-tone ladies' shoes, then that was their business. They would, of course, die. But that was of no interest to him. Mick nudged Gubmund who cleared his throat to speak.

'I hear you need someone to run messages.'

Mongo mulled this over and looked down at his expensive Adidas basketball boots. The closest he had come to playing basketball this year was hanging a first year on a fence by his underpants. The unfortunate basketball player had been left with the dilemma of whether to bear the discomfort until he was discovered, or risk the complete destruction of his waistband in an attempt to release himself. Mongo was the sort of a guy who gauged the success of such an action by how many laughs he got. He didn't do these things because he enjoyed them; he was not a sadist. He did them because he could, and that to him was reason enough.

'Right, you get to wear the shoes if you get a few things for me in town.' Mongo produced money and a list torn from a notebook and looked Gubmund in the eye.

'Anyone stops you, and you tell them you're collecting stuff for me. *Anyone.*'

Gubmund headed off to class and opened the list as he walked:

One packet of American Hard Gums.

One packet of Sugar Puffs.

Ten Major.

Ten Silk Cut Purple.

Two packets of green Rizla.

One packet of Mates from the chemist.

One packet of Juicy Fruit chewing gum.

One Wham Bar.

One Handball (Dunlop).

When he sat down, a priest was trying to impart the joy of geography. He pointed out the main cities of Brazil as the class became aware of the telltale shoes.

'Recife on de North East Coast is a major centre of commerce for de hinterland with a sugar cane processing industry ...'

'Check out the funky mammy brogues man!' said Minto, who had appointed himself the fashion arbiter of the class.

'Belo Horizonte is noted for its … are you lads listening to me at all?' said the priest reaching for his metre stick.

'Are there a lot of shoe shops in Brazil sir?'

'Well de leatherworking industry would be centred in de south. Why do you ask?'

'Well, I heard we are importing some mad looking shoes from the third world.'

The class erupted and the priest knew he had lost them again. Minto gave Gubmund the cut-throat gesture but was instantly corrected by a punch to the right kidney from Fucus. This outlined the fact that Gubmund now had the equivalent of diplomatic immunity: he was untouchable.

He walked out the gates at lunchtime going through the list. He picked up the sweets and fags at the newsagents where the convent girls hung out. They wore gabardine skirts accessorised with bubble gum and menthol cigarettes. He was keeping an eye out for the girl with the red hair who usually occupied this spot. She wasn't around, but two girls from home were. They looked at the bag in his hand.

'Where are you off to with all that stuff?'

'Food run for the boarders. It's my new job.'

'Why are you bothering with that shower?'

Gubmund pointed at the tan loafers.

'Oh right. If they were a bit smaller my mother would wear them.'

He would have waited around if he didn't have such a heavy schedule from Mongo. He bought the handball in the sports shop, then casually wandered into the chemist. He picked up the condoms. The girl behind the counter showed no reaction and took the offered note. She opened the till but was short of change so she opened the cash register at the other end of the counter. The door swung open and a couple of convent girls came in. He knew without turning around that the red-haired girl was one of them. He crept his hand over the packet on the counter but was too late.

'Good man Gubmund, it looks like you've a good weekend planned.'

'They aren't mine, I'm picking them up for lads at school.'

'That's what they all say ... what exactly are you going to do with the handball, or do I want to know?'

'It's the shoes, it all started with the shoes.'

'I'd say you'll be describing this to a psychiatrist in a few years.' The girl smiled, it was a pitying smile, but a smile nonetheless. Gubmund walked back up the town towards the school. There were none of the usual crowds around the gate. He was late.

He tried to speed up but the tan shoes were cutting into his ankles so he proceeded at a slow grimacing canter up the avenue. In a puff of Major smoke, a priest with wispy grey hair appeared from behind the statue of the school's founder. The statue was of some bishop from the previous century in a soutane and was universally known as 'Stoneskirt'. The priest in front of the statue was the dean and he was not shy about administering discipline when he saw fit. He usually went for a ringing slap to the ear but often used an uppercut for variety. He looked at the bag in Gubmund's hand curiously. The student paled, the last thing he wanted was a conversation about bringing prophylactics into the school grounds.

'You're late, have you got a reason?'

'I had to collect stuff for one of the boarders.'

'Really, we will have to see about that now won't we?'

'It's for Mongo, Mongo McPartland.'

The priest stepped back as if stung and gestured that Gubmund should be on his way. He went to his locker through the quiet corridors. As he opened the door, Mongo materialised beside him. He had a key in his hand.

'Any more just leave the stuff in there and I will collect it.'

'How did you get a key for my locker?'

Mongo held up a ring of keys and touched his nose. 'The only problem is keeping track of which one is which. Did you get the handball?'

Gubmund nodded and handed it to Mongo who hopped it off the floor a few times.

'There's a money game going on tonight and some fuckin' eejit put all the handballs on the roof.' Mongo scowled to indicate the culprit would be dealt with severely. 'I sent Fucus up to collect some but he's kind of useless. I bought this one as insurance, supply and demand you see.'

There was an elongated scream from the direction of the handball alleys followed swiftly by a thud. It looked like Mongo was going to have staff out on sick leave for a while. Gubmund went into his class and sat down at the back. People moved out of his way. In this place if you didn't fit in you needed to carry a big stick. Sticks didn't come much bigger than Mongo.

On the way out towards the bus, Minto asked Gubmund where he could get a pair of the shoes. 'The point is not moot, I must have the boots.' Mick laughed as Gubmund promised to have a look for a pair in a size eight.

'You'll be doing well to find another pair of those yokes.'

'The mother specialises in this stuff, there shouldn't be a problem.'

'We're gonna be rich, rich I tells ya!'

'Once Mongo doesn't go straight to the source on the wholesale market ...'

Gubmund lit one of Mongo's cigarettes as he got on the bus. He was too cool for school, much too cool.

Town of Fiction

by PAUL McMAHON

*Love is a town of fiction where the unrequited lover holds
lonesome authority. He only knows the middle of the streets,
not the endings or the beginnings. The turning point, the day
the tables turned, is somewhere behind – just where cannot
be remembered. He has a pied map of stitch-work memories
spread out over the bonnet of his mind. The attic of his
dream-house has been blown open to the elements – his gone
days of concentration are the babbled pages that flutter in the
rainy wind. He stalks through the old streets that never age.
'Tonight you will be with me somewhere better than the streets
of fiction,' he said to the two men crucified to his either side,
as they drove the nails through his hands. Who were those
two unrequited men nailed on either side of Christ and why
were they portrayed as extreme opposites, like an implanted
artificial dramaturgical trick? The three of them are on the hill
overlooking the town of fiction. All three of them have spent
their lives wandering its winding cobble-stoned laneways. I left
fiction to listen to them. The one in the middle was telling the
other two of a different town, somewhere invisible but real. An
agent from the town hall lanced the middle man in the side
and he fell silent. Other agents laughed, entwining irony into
a crown that they placed on his head and proclaimed him king
of fiction. It started to rain – or maybe it didn't – and I walked
back towards town. I was smiling. I didn't know why. Then it
began to rain. So it wasn't raining earlier. I was still smiling. It
wasn't raining – it was actually snowing. White snowflakes fell
and fell. The distant roofs turned white. I didn't look back to
the king of fiction on the hill flanked by two extremes but kept
walking towards the whitening town. The fluffy snow crunched
under my feet as I neared the city walls. I looked back to
my footprints in the snow but there were no footprints. I felt*

like Hansel, my footprints gone, disappeared into a landscape of snow-white breadcrumbs that led back to the hill where the three crosses were outlined against the grey sky. I turned towards fiction again. Written above the town gates of fiction it says: It is acceptance and not love that is evergreen amongst the deciduous. A bell tolled as I passed under the arch. I was still smiling. I didn't believe the man on the hill; people can make up anything when they are nailed to a cross. I signed my name on the scroll, once more in unrequited acceptance of my lonesome authority, and walked into town barefoot. The bell kept tolling or maybe it didn't, maybe it was just the clapper of joy ringing in the bell-dome of my head, because as I was on the hill listening to the three men speak of somewhere else invisible but real, I realised that if their nails were taken out all three would have run with joy; with hope, anticipation; with expectation; with hunger; with love; with burning love, like children in a playground, unrequited, back to the town of fiction.

The Count

by CONOR MONTAGUE

An explosion of white light signals a tremendous thump on the back of Ed's head. He floats momentarily in soft blackness, sounds sinking into a vacuum, teetering on the edge, before rolling gently over into a chasm. Eyes jerk open as he senses himself falling, blinding glare and noise increasing in intensity, like emerging at speed from deep water into the midday sun. Scuba-diving in the Andaman Sea – his honeymoon – decompressing as boats pass on the surface, engine noise dispersing into the blue. Silhouette overhead: featureless face in blinding halo.

ONE!

An operating theatre, surgeon leaning into his face, he battles the anaesthetic, fears the nothingness. Katie's face on hearing the news, voice pleading, reminding him of his promise. 'He has nothing left to prove ... why would he want to go back? Do her feelings not matter?' Tears fill deep cobalt-blue eyes as she realises the futility of her rant ... she knows that set jaw ... knows she'll be sitting at ringside consumed with fear, praying that the man who comes out of that ring will be the same man who walked in.

TWO!

A man: holding up two fingers. Flashes attack from all directions, sending tiny fluorescent sparks swirling upwards into all-consuming light. Inishmaan, summer-time, 1990, lying on the grass by the cliffs, stargazing as waves crash onto the rocks below ... dreaming of America ... the land of opportunity they said ... a fighter could do well there, with a bit of luck and a lot of talent.

THREE!

It's the referee. Ed struggles to focus. He's down, crowd roaring, voices infected with bloodlust. His head is heavy as an anchor on a ring that seems to be floating on the choppy swells west of Aran. Countless cameras flash, determined to record his weakness, to rejoice in his frailty as they mentally prepare the 'I told you so' headlines for the morning rags. He remembers the stinging jibes at the press conference, 'Do you think a man of your age can withstand the power of Tiger Lopez?' 'Why are you coming back?' 'Aren't you afraid of getting badly hurt?'

FOUR!

Ed rolls onto his right shoulder, using the momentum to swivel onto his knee. The arena spins, a mangled montage of speeding facial features. He's in the gym in Brockton, Goody Peroni sitting beside him on the apron, 'always take the count son, if you're hurt take the count.' He looks up into the animated face of a television commentator spitting an English accent into a microphone. 'He's down ... Ed Joyce, the Man of Aran, is down in the first round here in Madison Square Garden ... and he's hurt ... Joyce is hurt ... Tiger Lopez has one hand on the featherweight title.'

FIVE!

Running through the early morning, sucking icy air into starved lungs, vapour exhalations merging into the fingers of mist reaching up from the valley. Talking to himself, shouting, willing burning legs up steep slopes. Goody's voice: 'yo pegs gotta be independent son ... when yo brain is mush and yo sense all fucked-up ... yo pegs need to stand alone.'

SIX!

He sees the ref more clearly now, latex covered hands in front of crimson-speckled white shirt. He hears the crowd, feels the heat from the lights, smells sweat and blood and leather. He's in the gym, punching the bag as Goody shouts into his ear: 'last thirty seconds Ed ... finish strong son ... finish every round strong ... that's what the judges remember ... You think they gonna hand you that title?' Manny Packard answers from the other side ... 'no siree, ain't goin' handin' out no titles ... you gotta grab that motherfucka ... no doubt.' A mantra spreads through the gym as he pounds the heavy bag, steam rising around him, dispersed by flashing fists as sacred words coax the dregs of strength from deep inside. 'No doubt ... we ain't got no doubt.'

SEVEN!

It was an overhand right, never saw it coming ... too slow bringing back the jab. Caught cold ... he looks to Goody in the corner, struggling to focus on the job in hand. As their eyes lock and hold, Goody grins that crooked-toothed smile of his and nods. Ed smiles ... that was Tiger's best shot ... they both know it ... Tiger knows it too ... standing across the ring poised like a panther ... black muscular torso glistening ... eyes burning with the desire to beat a legend half to death in front of the world, to rip the still-beating heart from his chest, leaving a bloody corpse to slump onto the canvas, an unrecognisable battered shell of his former self.

EIGHT!

The Arena erupts as Ed Joyce stands to his feet, holding gloves up before him to signify his ability to continue. Twenty thousand Irish fans scream encouragement, invigorated by the prospect of more bloodshed, more pain, more drama acted out upon a brutal stage they themselves fear to tread. The referee looks deep into Ed's eyes as he rubs the 8oz leather mitts on his shirt. 'You alright, Ed?' Standing brings brief relapse. The room swirls around three referees. His legs are jelly and his mouth tastes like burnt enamel. He looks the middle one straight in the eye. 'Never been better.' Goody's Boston boom bellows from the corner, 'Hey Ed!' They lock eyes one last time as Goody calmly mouths the mantra, nodding his head sagely as if this whole scenario is part of ancient scripture, with his boy here to fulfil the prophecies of old … destined to achieve greatness one last time. Ed absorbs Goody's conviction with the cheers of the baying mob, takes a deep breath and smiles around his black gum-shield.

As the referee shouts 'box' and the crowd soars toward crescendo, a flicker of doubt flashes across the eyes of Tiger Lopez.

In His Shoes

by ALAN CADEN

The breeze at the seafront was much cooler. Not our seafront, but their one. Looking across the bay past wheeling gulls I could see our seafront, the old port where fishermen still came ashore with their dwindling hauls. Here, everything was clean and white, palm trees and tall hotels with glass and swimming pools. It was nearing sunset, and the tourists came out for the coolest part of the day, to walk hand-in-hand along the promenade, have something to eat, leave the kids (if they had any) back at the hotel and then go clubbing for the night. I was roasting, but couldn't take off my jacket.

'Whatever you do,' he ordered, 'don't stop, not even for a moment.'

'Yeah, yeah … I know.' I responded.

'Not even for a second! If you pause, you are lost.'

I was only half-listening to him. I was more concentrated on the strangely comforting jigging of my leg beneath the table, and on the plans in my head. I was aching to go.

'Idiot! I am serious! Listen!' he emphasised, grabbing me by the shoulder and squeezing my neck like Dr. Spock until I turned and looked at him. He used to always do that when we were kids. He transfixed me with his eyes, pinning me in my chair, until I pretended to come to my senses. I gulped nervously like I knew he wanted me to, and then stuttered in assent. He was relieved.

'Good. Good man. You know we're all behind you, don't you?'

I nodded again, eagerly. I knew he wasn't even that comfortable with this, so I wanted to make it easier on him.

'I know it's hard. But think of our mother …' he reasoned.

'Okay, Okay. I know exactly what to do. Seriously, there'll

be no fucking around. I promise you. I've done enough of that lately, haven't I?'

He stroked his extensive beard, and I took this as assent.

Indeed, I had fucked around quite a lot. In fact, that was the only reason I was here with my brother, who I hadn't talked to in over a year and who I considered to be one of the most simultaneously detestable and pitiable characters I had ever met. Him and his sagely tugging of the beard. If his big friends told him that picking hairs from your anus was sagely and devout, he'd do that. Still, it was those same big friends that were going to help me out of the tight spot I was in.

It was really the incident of the whore's shoes that brought all this about, although there had been other things: the gambling debts, the parking tickets, the bootleg alcohol.

You see, I had always been friendly with the whores of the Blue Baths ever since I ran errands for them as a teenager. Then I got big, one of them made a man of me, and I began to hang around there quite a lot, as a non-paying guest, you understand. I learned a lot in those long, lingering days without a touch of cloud or responsibility, in the break between the wars … Ah yes, the shoes …

Well, there was this one young thing, Leila, with dusky eyes and perfect handful-sized breasts, who I was particularly fond of. It so happened that when I awoke from her slender olive arms one morning, I couldn't find my trainers. They had been kicked under the bed in the heat of my impressive passion, and when I located them they were lying under the bed beside another pair of shoes. Now, I looked at them both and saw that the other shoes were an extremely expensive brand, and the gold bands on the laces had little *Gucci*'s engraved on them. A most distinguished pair of shoes indeed. Beside them, my tatty runners extended their frayed laces like the hands of beggars in mute supplication. Even beneath the bed, these new shoes shined, and I thought them more fitting for a playboy like me than my knock-off Adidas. A man with those shoes would be taken seriously. So, with my satisfied love-toy dozing in bliss and none the wiser, I slipped on the shoes and strode out of the Baths. They were most comfortable. I felt like a man with business.

Most comfortable, that is, until a couple of days later when I was working in the café along the tourist seafront – even us playboys must make ends meet, and it *was* an excellent place to meet ugly, but generous, foreign women. However, on this occasion, the table was not that of such a lady, but a large and self-important sweating mound of a man who had just booked a table for three. Being the only waiter serving the terrace that evening, I had the dubious honour of being at his beck and call.

'Boy!' he called me for this, and 'lazy!' for that. 'More coffee!' and 'this Pepsi is not cold!' so that he had me running in and out for one thing or another until I was so enraged I felt like pissing in his Pepsi and throwing it over his jowly bald head. When I came out with his water, I found him looking at my feet in a very curious manner.

'Boy' he said to me quietly. 'Where did you get those shoes?'

I knew they would be commented upon!

'In a shoe-shop, sir,' I replied in obsequious fashion. 'Where else?'

'Don't take that insolent tone with me, you upstart!' he growled and I smiled in inward satisfaction to see him perspire at my clever retort. 'In which shop, and when? Have you a receipt? I demand you to tell me now, you little turd!'

Anyway, we went on like this for a small while, him heaping threats and insults upon me, and me all the while riling him with smart comments and witty repartees. By now I began to suspect that his feet were somewhat more familiar with the shoes than were mine. Our exchange reached such a point that he could no longer stand my bluffing and laid his cards on the table.

'You are a filthy liar!' he said, 'and do you know how I know this? Because those shoes were custom-made for *me* in Syria – Damascus, in fact, and there is not a single pair like them in this city! Now will you tell me you got them from a shop, boy?' he stated triumphantly.

I was unaware that Mr. Gucci was from Damascus.

'No,' I answered meekly, 'but I *will* tell you that I stole them from a whore in the Blue Baths who said I had a cock twice the size of yours ... and that you should really see a doctor as quick as possible. Sir!'

I admit I may have taken slight liberties with the truth, but his reaction told me I was right, as I'm sure were my proportional measurements.

What neither of us noticed, however, in the heat of discussion, was that his two dinner-partners had arrived and were waiting patiently for our altercation to finish. Quite quickly, I deduced from the faces of the two, and from the man's startled look of a fish gasping for air, that it was his wife and child. I will not bore you here with the details of my incredible escape from the restaurant, but suffice it to say that the lumbering mound humiliated himself even more in front of a gathering crowd, as he swiped and lunged at my agile self while I heaped insult upon delightful insult onto his reddening head. I recall the look on his face as I jumped onto the bus, his rage beginning to blend with the realisation that he now had to face his wife. I laughed for the whole bus journey, and related the story to any who cared to listen.

I was slightly annoyed to find myself out of a job, as I rightly presumed, but it wasn't until I came home the next evening that I found out the full extent of my woes. My brother, who had assumed (unasked) the role of father in the house, greeted me at the door with a slap in the face and a religious tirade. When he eventually calmed down I got some sense out of him.

'You cursed, stupid fool! You selfish, sinful fickle playboy! Allah knows you never think of anyone else, do you?' he roared. And he continued in that vein. I was too distracted looking at Mother's sad, drawn face to tell him to get to the point. This was serious, and I have tried my utmost all my life to avoid serious.

'The man that you disrespected? Who you said those lies to in front of everyone?' His tone was accusatory and patronising as always and I tried to interrupt and tell him what had really happened but he was having none of it and silenced me with a sentence. 'That was Abu Nasr! Abu Nasr, you idiot! Do you know what that means? Do you?'

I did. I was chilled to the marrow. Mother looked at me as though she were already in mourning. My younger sister, Selima, who I loved so dearly, had thankfully been sent out of the house, but she would come to know of my disgrace before long.

Abu Nasr. Of course I knew him. Everybody in the city knew him. I had never seen him before, not even a picture, but his reputation was well enough known. Notorious gun-runner, militia leader, smuggler, drug-lord and ruthless murderer of any who crossed him. He was like the Godfather from the movies, but with neither the style nor honour. And I had crossed him. It was hard to equate that fat red-faced man with the notorious criminal, but it was he. At that very moment, the wind that had filled my sails, that had blessed me with a buoyant attitude and a happy life in this trouble-torn shithole, vanished completely.

My mother cried. My brother berated me, begged me to embrace Allah and pray to Him to find a way out of this mess. He waved the Qur'an in my face. Sura this and verse that. I said nothing. I considered that I had the cunning of Ala'ud'din but try as I might I could figure no way out of my predicament. And what was my predicament, exactly?

I came to find out in the coming days. Rumours of misfortune travel faster than the eagle himself. Not only had Abu Nasr decreed that I was to die, but for the sheer magnitude of the insult he had sentenced my family to death too. There could be no question of police or anything of the sort. They would probably be the ones to carry it out. My father alone was to be spared, he had said with Qur'anic humour, for no man can die twice. Abu Nasr was not a particularly religious man, but a man of violence and business, and so he had set a price on the non-execution of his revenge. It was a price far beyond any means that I or anyone else could come up with. It was a hopeless situation. We had nothing of value, not even the few rooms we lived in. Friends and relatives refused us any help, afraid to be associated with the debt if anything went wrong. None of my girlfriends answered their phones. I became depressed.

The days went on and we sought any and every means of escape from the sword that hung over our heads. It was hopeless. Until my brother came to me with a proposition which, he claimed, he didn't want to give me.

Now, I know that you may consider me reckless and selfish, and I would be the first to concur, but I am only reckless and selfish with my own life. I have never been malicious, and I never wanted anyone else to share in the consequences of my personality, least of all my mother and my sister. My mother, the most amazing person that I know, had raised us all through war and my father's death by denying herself everything. And my sister, a sunburst of joy who could be what our mother had never been able to be, who could leave this place and go to France, or America. Even my brother and the religion that compensated for his lack of confidence, though I knew the death-sentence wouldn't touch him. I couldn't possibly ask them all to pay the price for my stupidity.

You may think that I was even stupider still to agree to my brother's proposition, but perhaps you know how it feels when you are in deep trouble from which there is no way out, and then someone offers you a chance to do something to atone for it. It may not be the right thing, but it is something. Maybe you don't know how this feels, and then I say you are indeed blessed, my friend, and may you never know it. But let me tell you what you would do: you would take that escape route, though it be the last thing you want to do, you understand me? You know you would. Or at least you know you should.

So my brother told me there was something that needed to be done, something important. He didn't really spend much time at home anymore. Since our father died he had taken to spending more and more time at the *madrasah*. This made my mother happy, because it took two burdens off her shoulders; she didn't have to provide for another mouth in the household, and she didn't have to worry about another troublesome son like me. But I don't think she was fully aware that it wasn't all praising Allah, discussing theology and helping the poor that they were up to there.

And if there was one person who could call off Abu Nasr's dogs, it was their leader, the Sheikh. But he needed something done. Nothing for nothing. Theirs is not the God of unconditional charity.

'Good. You know where to go? Exactly? You have looked at the map? You know what to do? Right, come into the back ...' I could sense now that my brother was beginning to get uneasy with the situation. Whether it was pangs of conscience for his younger brother or his warped excuse for morality, I cannot say with any certainty.

In the back room of the internet café, I saw the real movers. My brother merely owned the donkey. They recorded me with a digital camera as I gave the prepared speech, with banners behind that said 'Allah is Great' and 'Death or Victory'. They didn't think the two were mutually exclusive. I sat on a three-legged stool behind an old school desk, wondering how many others had sat here, but I spoke with such conviction and feeling that they must have thought I was Mohammed reborn. Once those formalities were out of the way, it was straight down to business.

'Here. Try it on. How does it feel?' one of the men asked me. 'Make sure it is comfortable. You don't want to look shifty.'

'Well, it's no Hilfiger.' I replied, which drew no laughs, only blank stares. 'Yes. It is good. Heavy, but good.'

And then they ran through the details once again with me, for the hundredth time. I answered obediently, making sure to seem neither too confident nor too nervous. Yes, I knew exactly the route I would take. Yes, I knew how long to wait. No, I didn't have any doubts. Yes, I knew how many virgins would be waiting for me (though it wasn't as many as I had disqualified from that category in my short life). Yes, I had the mobile they had given me. Yes, it was charged. Yes, I had memorised the number to ring from the mobile to detonate it.

Did I have any last questions or wishes?

I wanted to know who they thought they were, what role they were playing, what life they considered this to be, but I knew it wouldn't go down well, so instead I said firmly:

'I have the Sheikh's word that my family will be taken care of? Not your word, but the Sheikh's? On the name of Allah and the Prophet? Yes? Good. Then I am ready.'

My brother thought it time to show some brotherly feeling, and he clasped my hand.

'Haroun, you know it is for the good of Allah and your people that you do this?' I wanted to tell him that Allah had nothing to do with any of this.

'I am so proud of you,' he said, and pumped my hand while he smiled at the other men. I felt sick.

I put on the jacket and I left the café. My shoes trod comfortably on the cracked pavement. Dogs barked and men shouted their prices in a vacuum. I took a bus to the marina, to the tourist promenade. On the bus I sweated profusely in the midday heat. My gel ran into my eyes. I felt everyone was looking at me, commenting under their breath about how suspicious I looked. Two policemen got on near the station. Underneath their dark glasses I could sense them observing me. I couldn't take it. I got off at the Hotel Mediterranean. The promenade was packed. Here there was flesh on view. Here there was no rule except that of spend and have fun. Three small Western children threw a Frisbee back and forth through the crowds while their mother chased them. The sea sparkled. Luxury yachts bobbed lazily while their owners sipped cocktails on the deck. Lobster and fish and lamb sizzled, and holidaymakers tucked into five-course meals with wine. On my side of town, old women scratched each other's eyes as they queued at the well.

I looked at the water, and the wide sunset. Can't I just throw the jacket in there? What would happen? The mother of the children nudged against me and apologised as she set off in pursuit of her little terrors. A young couple looked at me to avoid meeting each other's eyes. I walked to the end of the pier. I looked around, wondered if they had someone watching me.

A family walked along down the pier. The father fat and sunburnt, his wife alternately smiling and frowning as she looked at a map. The teenage daughter bored and sullen, her little brother awe-struck at all the new sights to take in.

As they approached, my doubts bubbled and burst. I started to unzip the jacket.

But they must have known because at that moment they rang me.

There are no virgins here.

Last Orders

by CONOR MONTAGUE

Harry Barrett swings his black Audi TT into the loading bay outside Jury's Inn. He sits watching a chaotic Quay Street. The rain has stopped, and the cobbled road glistens under the streetlights, reflecting refracted images of weekend revellers as they migrate between the twelve or so watering holes servicing Galway's west-end.

Two long-haired teenage girls stagger from the direction of the Spanish Arch, bare bellies bobbling over belt-sized mini skirts. As they cross in front of the car, the shorter one lurches forward and spews a dark stream of puke onto the soaked pavement, sending a volley of splatters up along the imitation leather of her companion's fuck-me boots. Harry sits watching her white ass gleaming at him from either side of a black G-string as her friend struggles to hold back blonde curls with her left hand, the right one choking a bottle of Buckfast.

'That's it Jacinta, get it out of ya loveen, you'll feel better.'

Harry watches, strangely aroused by the scene, the low sporty profile of the TT gifting him a prize vantage point. The other girl takes a swig from the bottle, lights from passing traffic sparkling in her gold hoop earrings as she tilts her head back. She spots Harry observing from the car.

'What the fuck are ya lookin' at ya filthy fucker ... mind your fuckin' bizznis like ...'

Jacinta turns to look and slips, falling flat on her arse in her own puke, legs splayed wide, left boob popping out from under a belly-top displaying the caption *Girls Just Wanna Have Fun*. Her friend's left hand is entwined in her hair, and the momentum of the fall forces her to lurch sideways and trip over Jacinta, falling face first onto the soaked pavement. Harry starts the car, taking one last look at the exhibition of young flesh laid out upon the cold concrete before slowly pulling out, laughing. 'Classy chicks,' he says, catching his own eye in the rear-view mirror. 'Classy fucking chicks.'

He drives around the corner, keeping left onto Cross Street, through the junction and past St. Nicholas' Church, where he finds a parking space along Market Street. He walks back down towards the bar. Two men are squaring up to one another outside Supermac's, wide-eyed, spouting trash-talk as they struggle to stay within the clutches of the friends holding them back, each afraid to commit to the physical, like drunken caricatures of stage Irishmen in a Victorian farce. Harry turns left up Mainguard Street to avoid the hassle, turning right into High Street and striding through the madness that lurches towards him from all directions. A middle-aged couple are having a heated argument outside *Murphy's Bar*. A short stocky man with an unruly mop of black hair is pleading with his partner to calm down. His blue check-shirt is open to the waist, leaving a perfectly round beer belly exposed to the night. A cigarette glows in stumpy yellowed fingers as he spreads arms wide, gazing into her haggard face, contorted with an anger that chisels a network of trenches into her skin, caked with make-up that betrays the optimism of early evening. Huge tits quiver on swollen mid-riff as she spits venom, leaping briefly from their resting place as she lands a gunshot slap onto the red blotchy cheek of her lover.

'YOU DON'T LOVE ME VINNIE!' she screams, before turning on her heel and marching up the street, her black leather skirt struggling to contain a backside that bears little resemblance to the one it had been bought to accentuate. Vinnie reels back on his heels and takes a moment to compose himself. He turns to the assembled crowd of smokers with a broad grin and winks, before shouting after her,

'OF COURSE I LOVE YA MARY, I'M RIDIN' YA AMN'T I?'

His audience bursts out laughing. Harry can't help but smile, despite the number of times he has heard this staple of pub humour. Vinnie certainly has a point. Harry continues down the street and pauses at the door to tell Josh what had been said, and check if there had been any incidents during the night. 'So far so good Boss,' says Josh, chuckling at Vinnie's eloquence. 'All quiet on the Western Front.' Harry nods approvingly and walks in through the doors of *Harry's*.

Raymo flicks the lights off and on three times. By the time he turns around they are four deep at the bar, pushing and shoving and clamouring over one another. He surveys the mayhem momentarily before shifting into gear, working his way down the counter with speed and accuracy. He spots Harry enter the bar as he places three Guinness on the counter.

Harry is tall, immaculately presented. His black chinos are creased, and his cream coloured Tommy Hilfiger pullover contrasts perfectly with his tan. The hesitant stride of the street shifts to a swagger as he walks through the door. He pauses to peruse the scene, slipping his wedding ring off his finger and into the top right pocket of his pants. He singles out people to be avoided. Billy Jackson will try and tap him for cash; Melanie's fiancé Keith seems to suspect something; Charlie Roberts will bore him to death, but has a couple of nubile fillies pinned against the wall so may be an option later. It's easy to impress with Charlie as a wing man. First things first.

Bob Marley's *Could You Be Loved?* kicks in, sending a tremor of excitement up the collective spine. The spectacle of drunken Irish people dancing to Caribbean rhythms with such reckless abandon and lack of timing brings a smile to Raymo as he takes the next order. He waves up at Paddy behind the decks.

Dawn flinches as Harry walks to the bar, and looks down into the pint of Carlsberg she's filling. Her face reddens as he leers over ... she can still taste him, still taste the salty residue, like a rotten oyster lodged halfway down her throat. She shudders as she recalls the hands on the back of her head, pulling her down, forcing her to swallow. Why had she stayed for that drink? She had been warned enough times, seen it all herself, and still she fell for Harry's bullshit, slamming shots until he had carried her home laughing and joking – all harmless fun.

She'd never forget the look on his face as he left her bedsit, or how it made her feel.

The shirts are shouting at Raymo, varying tones and inflections in an attempt to win his favour, panicking in case they might be excluded from this final frenzy.

'Raymo ... Raymo ... Hey Raymo ...'

'Ray, over here, Ray, over here Ray.'

'Two Heineken and a Smirnoff Ice there Raymo, when ya get a chance like.'

Raymo disperses drink every bit as quickly as Dawn, Des and Lucy combined down at the far end of the bar. He works his way along the counter, missing nobody, until he reaches the pillar, then repeats the exercise. No amount of shouting or jostling shifts him from the clinical methodology that has served the thirsty so well over the years. Nobody is left behind when Raymo's in command, but still they panic, ever fearful of a first time.

Harry moves to where Dawn is serving, sliding up to Séamus Kelly, offering him a drink before shouting over the counter.

'Dawn, two Guinness there please!'

She feels his eyes grope her as she fills the pints, leaving them to settle before turning to another customer. He nudges Seamus and nods towards her, bringing a blush to her cheeks. Their laughter grates across her fragility like wet chalk on a fresh blackboard, sending an involuntary tremor through her perfect form as she swallows her shame and almost chokes on the memory.

'Have one yourself, love,' as he hands her fifteen Euro, brushing her wrist with his fingertips before taking his pint, slapping Seamus on the back and moving further into the mêlée of closing time. She fights back tears as she opens the till, cursing her stupidity. Seven Euro, that was the payment, the sole gesture towards services rendered. Seven Euro – the cheapest whore in town. She looks towards Raymo as he twirls and dances, laughing with the customers, muscular arms glistening in the heat as he fills pints. Dawn prays that he hasn't heard about last night, but knows prayers are futile.

Harry's boasts will spread like syphilis in a brothel, making her just one more notch on his Gucci belt.

Des gives Dawn a gentle nudge with his elbow as he muscles in on the till. She's not herself tonight, short of the pace required to fuel the furnace across the counter. He wonders if she indulged in a smoke during her break; she certainly appears disoriented.

'Alright there, Dawn?'

'What? Oh! Yeah, just a little tired, sorry.'

'Nearly there now ... nearly there.'

He turns towards a short red-faced man shouting at him from the corner, but not before stealing a glance down along the small of Dawn's back as she turns from the till. A scarlet thong stretches up over low-cut jeans that only a girl in the slender prime of youth can get away with. He fights the urge to grab her, to twirl her around and plant a kiss that will melt her heart, make her realise that he's the only man she can ever love.

She's out of his league. Des is too old, too unsuccessful for a girl like Dawn, and he knows it. That doesn't stop him dreaming though, or conjuring up her image while engaging in acts of solitary perversion. The red-faced man catches his eye.

'Wouldn't mind a bit of that myself.'

Des nods agreement.

'What'll it be?'

'A Long Island Iced Tea and a White Russian!'

'Sorry, we're not doing cocktails at the moment ... can I get you anything else?'

The chorus shout in at Des.

'Four Guinness there before you finish, good man.'

'Les! Les! When you're ready like.'

Des nods at the crowd and looks back to the customer, eyebrows raised.

'What do ya mean you're not doing cocktails?'

'Sorry dude, it's too busy at the mo, can I get you anything else?'

He glares at Des, beady black eyes set so close together

that it's a safe bet his parents were blood relatives.

'Can I speak to the manager please?'

'No you can't speak the manager, piss off and stop wasting my time.'

'What? *What*? Do you know who I am? I'm a good friend of the owner I'll have you know.'

'Great, you can get him yourself then.'

Des turns to the next customer and takes an order for three Gin and Tonics before turning to the optics. The crowd, sensing that Cocktail-Boy is surplus to requirements, squeeze him out from the counter as he shouts an eclectic selection of obscenities, all rendered harmless by the loud music.

'Ray…three Guinness there before you finish, good man … and one for yourself.'

Raymo looks up at the smarm merchant. It's Johnny Gavin, belligerent block head protruding from the open neck of an Irish rugby jersey, collars upturned, worn in a manner that suggests a scrum is to take place at any second. Glistening globules of sweat gather around a hair-line that seems to be retreating from his bullshit. Raymo has noticed Johnny during the night, in and out to the toilet at fifteen minute intervals like a man with a bladder problem.

Harry approaches the counter. Raymo has twelve Guinness settling, and is putting together an order of three vodkas – two with ice – a Gin and Tonic, Havana Club with Coke and a slice of lime – the seven year-old stuff – two Heineken, one Carlsberg and a Diet Seven-Up with ice and lemon. He barks from the left.

'Raymo! Raymo!'

Raymo ignores him but knows he won't go away. Harry has spotted a flaw in his diamond and wants to make it clear to his right hand man. Raymo completes the order as Harry bristles with impatience.

'Raymo! Raymo!'

Raymo hands out the Diet Seven-Up. 'That'll be €36.30 please … Cheers.'

'Keep the change, Ray.'

'Thank you.'

Raymo takes the €40 and throws it into the till before giving himself a quick wipe with a tea towel and dancing back to the end of the counter where, at this stage, Harry is bouncing with frustration.

'Raymo!'

Raymo catches the eye of Ashling; she's a good regular, needs to be looked after.

'Can I get a Smirnoff Ice please?'

Raymo turns and grabs the bottle from the cooler, popping the cap and looking over at Harry as he takes a tenner from Ashling.

'Alright there Harry?'

He turns from the till and moves on to Enda, one of the soccer posse that invades the bar every Saturday night, dressed head to toe in bad attitude. He hands Aisling her change.

'Four Guinness.'

Harry finds room beside Enda and squeezes into the counter. 'Raymo, there's a load of glasses need collecting up the back.'

'What?'

Raymo moves onto the next customer while Enda's Guinness settle. He leans over towards him so he can hear the order above the music. Paddy's playing a remix of Dinah Washington's *Is you is, or is you ain't, my baby?* Raymo turns to the optics, dancing as he fills two vodkas, wagging his ass as he adds ice to the glasses, before doing a little twirl, placing the glasses on the counter, sliding down a bottle of lime, taking the note and doing another twirl back to the till. He looks up at Paddy behind the decks, who catches his eye and indicates a need for beer with a smile. Raymo puts on another Guinness and leaves it to settle as he tops up Enda's four pints and places them in front of him, taking the money from his hand as Harry grabs him by the wrist.

'Did you not fucking hear me? There's a load of glasses need collecting up the back.'

Raymo twists his left hand in a circular anti-clockwise motion until he is holding Harry's wrist and pulls him towards him. Harry, caught off balance, stumbles two steps down the counter until he is face to face with Raymo, bravado struggling for breath.

'Then go up the back and collect the fucking things, I'm busy.'

He turns the wrist slightly, locking Harry's arm at the elbow, and pushes, sending him careening back through the cronies he was trying to impress.

He throws Enda's money into the till and moves onto the next customer. 'Alright Miriam, what can I get you?'

Harry shakes himself, laughs for the public gallery and heads towards the front of the bar. As he walks through the limestone arch, he is accosted by Mr. Long Island Iced Tea, and, uncharacteristically, gets backed into a corner.

'Harry, how's it goin?'

'Alright ...'

'Simon! Simon Ferguson, I met you at the Galway Races last year ... in the Champagne tent ... at Sonny Molloy's table.'

Harry gives a half-hearted impression of recognition. 'Ah Simon, how are you ... listen I have to ...'

'Jesus that Sonny is some operator ha, six pubs he has now ya know, six pubs ... and him a Monivea man.'

The bar-staff are evacuating the bar, ignoring the few desperate souls that were too drunk or stupid to realise it was closing time. Harry tries to catch Dawn's eye but she doesn't look his way, walking out into the fresh air with head bowed. He should have stayed longer last night, shagged her again before he left. He's dragged back to reality by Simon Ferguson's incessant whine in his ear.

'He told me to fuck off you know.'

'What?'

'Your barman, he told me to fuck off.'

Harry perks up. 'Was it Raymo?'

'What?'

'Was it Raymo? Your man down there.'

Harry points down to where Raymo leans nonchalantly on the counter, chatting to Dermot Egan.

'No, it was Les.'

'Les?'

'Yeah Les ... over there.' He points to where Des is watching from the hatch at the end of the counter, smiling at the earful Harry is getting.

'Ah *Des* ... I seriously doubt that he told you to fuck off ... eh ... what did you say your name was?'

'Simon, and yes he did ... all I did was ask him for two drinks, he refused, and when I asked for a reason, he told me to fuck off. Now, I'm sure you'll agree Harry, that's no way to treat a good customer.'

'And were they finished serving?'

'No, this was before they finished ... I'm not leaving without a full apology.'

'You're not leaving ...'

'Without a full apology ...'

Harry looks long and hard at Simon. 'Hang on a minute and I'll check it out'.

He walks over to Des, leaving Simon mumbling to nobody in particular, seemingly aghast at the level of injustice still prevalent in modern society. It doesn't take Harry long to return.

'You asked for a Long Island Iced Tea and a White Russian.'

'Yes, two drinks.'

'A Long Island Iced Tea and a White Russian ... at closing time ... on a Saturday night. Where do you think you are exactly?'

'I'm in a bar, and I expect to get the drinks I order ...'

'Who are you with?'

'What?'

'Who is the second drink for?'

Simon stops and looks around, wearing a confused expression that implies that he can't quite remember what his companion looks like, or why she would possibly leave his side. He feels Harry's eyes on him and regains some of his composure.

'It doesn't matter who the other drink was for ... I'm a customer and expect to be treated with respect, not told to fuck off when I ask for a drink.'

'He told you to *piss* off.'

'What?'

'He told you to piss off ... you asked for two cocktails, he explained that he was too busy, you got stroppy, and he told you to piss off ... no big deal really.'

'No big deal? No big fucking deal? Have you any idea how to run a business? I'll have you know ...'

Simon pokes Harry in the chest just as Josh materialises behind him, a scowl distorting his tattooed Maori features. He grabs the collar of Simon's shirt with a hand so huge replicas of it could be sold as novelty items at wrestling events. Simon's yelps can be heard outside.

'Keep your hands off me ya overgrown ape, do you know who I am ... I make more in a day than you make in a month ... call the guards, call the fucking guards ... assault, I'll have you for fucking assault.'

Josh comes in from the front door and laughs across at Des.

'Instant asshole ... just add alcohol.'

Des smiles and shakes his head.

'Tell me about it.'

Simon's sudden departure injects a sense of urgency into the stragglers and the bar is clear within ten minutes. A few young girls linger with Harry's group of weekend mates, intoxicated by flattery, and talk of property, and expensive holidays and promises of time spent together beyond the couple of hours it takes the beast to have his way and discard her with his used condom. Harry latches on to two of them, Bethany and Jane. They've been weekend regulars for the past few months, since they've been legal. The men check their 3G phones at thirty-second intervals. Raymo nudges Des as he passes.

'Look at those fucks and their phones, what the fuck are they at? Checking in case a world leader needs late-night advice?'

Des looks over at the shirts as he places empties face down onto the wash-tray. 'Not at all Ray, it's the GPS they're keeping an eye on. If you don't know where you are, then you can't be sure of where you're going ... just good business my friend.'

Raymo laughs as Des pops the tray into the dishwasher and switches it on, and watches Harry motion to the two girls. The three walk towards the back office as Johnny Gavin regales the chorus with yet another heroic tale.

They return five minutes later with a spring in their step, the two girls babbling incessantly as Harry struts out just behind them, a claw on each tender loin. The smell of farts and stale drink is replaced by that of soap and bleach as the staff kick into gear, clinking glass their soundtrack for the thirty minutes it takes to restore cleanliness to the room. Lucy gets caught to serve Harry's associates while trying to clean behind the bar, each making a show of buying her a drink, like they're single-handedly erasing the debt of a third-world country.

Raymo puts Thievery Corporation on at low volume as they sit for their staff drinks. He catches Harry staring at him from his position between Bethany and Jane. Their chatter has gotten progressively louder and faster over the past thirty minutes. Raymo can hear an animated discussion about the latest *Big Brother* eviction and smiles at the thought of Harry having to listen to this inane banter. Nothing short of a spectacular *ménage à trois* is worth this suffering. He catches Dawn watching from the end of the bar and smiles down at her, throwing his eyes to heaven. He picks up his pint with the intention of joining her but Paddy plonks himself down and immediately launches into one of his 'you won't believe this' stories.

There's loud laughter from the shirts as Johnny Gavin kicks a punch line into touch to much back slapping and high-fives. Sweat runs in rivulets over his UV tan, soaking his rugby shirt around the neck-line. He scurries to the toilets to powder his nose as Brendan Fitz gets a round in, boring Lucy with bullshit as he adds a tray of shots to the order: Jägermeister all round.

Des quietly skins up in the corner, joined by Josh, who shows his appreciation of Des' wisdom by putting a pint-bottle of cider in front of him.

Harry touches Bethany gently on the arm and whispers into her ear, watching Raymo carefully, like a dog gnawing a bone in the presence of a rival.

'Listen babe, I'll be back to you in a minute ... there's a bit of business I have to take care of.'

He stands up, shaking his head in resignation. The two girls watch as he walks slowly towards Raymo, shoulders back, arms positioned as if he's carrying two buckets of water, patent black shoes loud on the wet timber floor. The conversation dies proportionally with each step, and all eyes are on Harry as he stands facing Raymo, who is sitting on a high stool, head bowed as he listens to Paddy spin a yarn, both oblivious to the silence. Harry stands over Raymo with clenched fists as Paddy delivers a punch-line with a giggle. He taps Raymo on his side, harder than necessary. Raymo doesn't look up, just leans towards Harry as he drinks from his glass.

'Raymo! RAYMO!'

Raymo glances at Harry sideways, saying nothing, before leaving his pint on the shelf and slowly turning on his stool to face him. 'What?'

The tone is casual, his face expressionless. Harry, mindful of his audience, swells up slightly as he looks down at his manager, sniffing hard to swallow acrid snot before continuing.

'When I tell you to do ...'

There's a flash of movement and Harry staggers backwards, a bloody mush where his vulture beak used to perch. He has no idea what just happened, nobody does. He looks down at his blood-soaked shirt, wondering where the crimson is flowing from. All chatter suspended as he staggers drunkenly in a little circle, looking back towards the two girls before attempting to focus on Raymo through teary eyes which are already shrinking back into the swelling. He steadies himself, and again looks at the blood dripping down onto the floor, transfixed by the sight as his right hand makes a futile attempt to stem the deluge. He is still looking down, wobbling like a rubber man when Raymo stands from his stool and walks over to him, unleashing an over-hand right that splits the left-hand side of Harry's face vertically from the centre, like worn corduroy across a fat man's arse.

The atmosphere can be tasted, viscous awkwardness with a dollop of shock and a pinch of subtle satisfaction. Harry lies where he lands, beside the two sweethearts, propped up against a pillar, lopsided with limbs askew and eyes glazed, like a rag doll discarded by a bored child. Blood flows from his bust nose and face onto the timber floor, quickly forming a dark, sticky pool that slowly creeps outwards, as does the warm yellow puddle around his crotch. There's no movement from Harry for thirty seconds, then he blinks slowly and tries to move, slipping down the pillar onto his left side, coughing up bloody phlegm and a tooth that rattles across the floor and spins momentarily beneath a table. All eyes are drawn to this fairy's bounty, seduced by the surreal image.

Jane and Bethany cry, but not for Harry. The shock of seeing the man with everything reduced to a man with nothing in the space of four or five seconds is too much for their young minds to comprehend. They cry for something far more heartbreaking than a man beaten half to death; they cry for something lost, devoured by an insanity they want no part of. Raymo turns towards them, eyes sparkling with adrenaline, blood dripping from his right fist. He looks like he's about to say something but decides against it, instead switching his gaze to Harry squirming on the floor in his own blood and piss. He smiles down at him before turning towards the back door. 'I'll catch up with ya later, Paddy.'

The girls' sobbing can be heard above the low music as he leaves. Dawn leaps off her stool and grabs her jacket. 'Raymo ... hang on there.'

She runs, heels clacking as she catches up, grabbing Raymo by the hand as they both exit into the early-morning darkness.

Antemortem

by AIDEEN HENRY

Carthage awoke at dawn on the day of his death. He showered, then dry-shaved by touch. He reheated porridge and sat out on the back step to eat. Carthage was a tall man with a mop of raven-black hair, a lantern jaw and a wiry frame. 'A dishwasher is a beautiful thing,' he whispered, as he reached in to unclip both rotating arms. He ran the tap water through the centre holes and watched the spouts of water coming out each end, like a child spilling water out of its mouth after punching both cheeks. He rinsed the filter then clicked it back into place, flush. He had a similar ritual with the miners' lamps he polished as a child in Arigna. As he worked, time stood still and his movements slowed, so it was more of a caress than a duty.

He left the house and walked to the tube station where he bought *The Roscommon Herald*. He got off at Ealing and made his way to the hospital.

'Howya Carthage? Anything new at home?' Josie, a matronly Cork woman smelling of Juicy Fruit, greeted him from the pathology office. Carthage smiled his crinkly smile, his conversation-dodger, and kept walking.

Once changed into blue scrubs, he reviewed the morning's list: two BIDs, one hanging, and infant twins. He moved to the first body brought in dead and started to work. He moved quickly each time he peeled back the layers of a body. In each there was something the pathologist wanted him to find: the clot lodged in a heart or brain artery, the broken neck vertebra of a hanging victim, waterlogged lungs in a suspected drowning, or the puncture-wound tracking a knife's insertion through the rib space, through the sack around the heart, reaching its inner silken lining. These were not what Carthage was looking for. As he weighed the heart, lungs and brain and noted his findings, his pace slowed. Stephanie often walked past the glass-block wall, click clack, click clack. 'That's all I need, an attractive woman. They're a bloody curse.'

He moved on to the twins. They were wrapped together in an orange fleece blanket. Reflexively, he put his little finger inside each of the tiny fists, as though they would grip him back. They were dressed in yellow woollen hand-knitted suits with buttons of different plastic fruits, little pixie hats with silver bells on them and laced bootees. He undressed them carefully and folded their clothes and unsoiled nappies onto a chair. Then he lifted their fleece blanket, folded it and pushed his face into it and breathed it in. Other people's homes and the smells that belong there. He laid the twins out like two pinned butterflies and carefully made the incisions so the pathologist could get to work. It was only with infants that you had to take great care. Their bodies were held and hugged up to the last before being placed in the coffin.

Next he moved onto the hanging. He looked into the man's face. Whatever had driven him to it was long gone. He looked mellow, as though he might stretch, take a deep breath and at any moment shout, 'Jesus, what's keeping ye? Will ye get a move on?'

Carthage took down the drill and started to bore the dead man's skull. He removed the brain and weighed it, then moved on to open the chest and abdomen. The pathologists wore masks while they worked. Carthage didn't bother, the smell of innards, animal or human, were of no consequence to him. Through the open window he smelled cigarette smoke and stopped working. As he stripped off his gloves and apron and washed his hands, he remembered two things about Marie he loved most: the sweet thread of tobacco that his tongue invariably found in some crevice of his mouth after leaving her, and the soft curve at the top of her leg where her thigh muscle attached to her hip bone. A small pad of flesh quivered there when she moved. He loved to rest his head on her stomach and run his fingertips over where firm muscle met with soft flesh. Lying there felt like home.

He walked down the corridor, past the open door of the packed staff room. Inside the back door, with the press of a button, the coffee machine spat into a beige plastic cup. Outside, he lit up. Sanjeet, a small man in his sixties, with pianist's hands, sad eyes and a limp, smoked in silence. Each man nodded briefly at the other then looked away. They could have been outside a church in Mohill on a warm spring Sunday, studiously ignoring the priest's request, audible through the packed open door, to show each other the sign of peace.

Each day Carthage opened his lunchbox and unwrapped the same piece of tinfoil with his sandwich inside. Lunch today was two slices of soda bread with lumps of smoked ham, scallions and mayonnaise. When he had finished he left, biting on a red apple as the others arrived. He walked across the hospital football pitch into the woods and lay on a mossy bank beside the stream. He looked up at the sun through the leaves. Marie smelt of popcorn. It wasn't from her face cream or make-up. He had checked them. It was from deep inside her. He could find it in her exhaled air as she lay asleep beside him and he moved in close to rebreathe her. It wafted from her pores in the heat. He looked down at the shadows made by the leaves on his hands, which were like shadows that move across the bottom of the wash-basin when suds float along the surface. This reminded him of a cloud's shadow tacking along the side of Ben Bulben on a windy day.

He left the woods and detoured to Davy's bookies before returning to the lab.

'Hello Irish, what can I do you for?' Pat grinned.

'Two pound each way on Birch Rider. The four o'clock.'

Pat took the money and gave him his docket. He was a rotund man with a ginger beard and fish-like blue eyes with long blond eyelashes.

'Done. Will you be in *Flanagan's* for one later? Marty's coming down for the night. We'll be there after nine.'

'Probably, see you so.'

Carthage spent the afternoon working on sections of the organs he had removed, taking slices at angles that best showed the cause of death. Stephanie click-clacked in and out, transferring specimens for staining to the lab upstairs. She was a buxom woman in her late thirties, the kind who assaults the senses with strong perfume and a tendency to stand too close. She reminded him she was having a hen-party that night after work. The more she crowded Carthage, the more he withdrew, to the point that now he didn't meet eye contact or reply.

His final job that day with Sanjeet was to stitch closed the rib cages, chests, abdomens and skulls as neatly as possible. At five o'clock they went for their last cigarette of the day. Sanjeet's long toes curled the grass, combing it, as he spoke.

'Two years I have left here in this dung-hole. My wife, she loves it. But in my heart I am still in Thakor. Everyday my mind is visiting the market and is breathing in the curries along with the putrid smells. Two more years, if God is willing.' The two men's eyes met and held, then Carthage looked away.

He bought two fillet steaks, a head of white cabbage and new potatoes. Then he took the bus. At the doorway beside *Flanagan's* he climbed the metal stairs, the tips of his shoes ting-tinging and the plastic food bag swishing against the metal railing. He rang the doorbell. After a few minutes he put a key in the lock and let himself in. The apartment was dark, smelling of wine and dope. He opened the curtains and the windows. In the kitchen he set the cabbage and potatoes boiling, then washed the frying pan, dried it and spilled rock salt onto it and laid the two steaks to cook on top. Tariq lay sprawled on the bed, his face obscured by his long hair. A beam of light from the evening sun lit up one buttock and a thin blackhaired leg. Carthage bent over, kissed him on the back of his neck, slapping the bare buttock.

Tariq rolled around surprised and wiped saliva from his chin. His eyes were blood-shot. In the kitchen Carthage whistled, listened to the racing news on Radio 1, then turned it off, and listened to Tariq sing in the shower.

Flanagan's was a comfortable pub until the new owners replaced the Formica and bubbled glass. Now it looked more like a stage-set for the Abbey. Despite this, the regulars continued to drink there. Mike, a red-faced brickie with a fading sunburn line on his neck, carrots for fingers and a lisp, was seated at the bar with his pint and chaser. He regaled Tariq behind the bar with his victorious stories, the theme always his ingenuity, the great man he was in fooling the Englishman. Tariq's attention was on the function room at the back where screams of laughter and singing were heard each time the door opened. Outside, Igor and his two Ukrainian friends sat like sentries, drinking lager. On the other end of the bar, two young Bengali men dressed in suits were deep in conversation. Carthage was smoking, leaning against the wall while Pat and Marty played pool. The pool cue was like a talking stick; each took their turn to speak before taking a shot. Marty was telling a story about an M1 motorway rescue call-out he had done that day.

'So he says to me, "You're rippin' us off mate, that's double you are chargin' for petrol." So I says, "I'm not your mate. Take it or leave it. I'm not here for the good o'me health. Like it or lump it." Fuckin' Pakis.'

'What did he say to that?' Pat grinned.

'Well, he went back to the car. You shoulda seen it. His wife, all meek, like, but his mother, she bawled him out of it. He paid in the end, though. No choice. What do they expect? Everythin' for nothin'?'

Carthage watched Tariq as he served pints to the two young men. When they took their seats again Tariq caught his eye and Carthage looked away.

The function room door opened and women teetered out. They wore pink hair bands with fluffy antennae and flashing lights.

Josie marched to the middle of the room and set down a high stool.

'Right. It's Stephanie's last time in here a single woman so we'll have a kiss, a nice orderly kiss now, from every man in the room. Form a queue lads.'

Stephanie swaggered over to the stool, in a bright red dress with a plunging neckline, jingling bangles, patterned black tights and stilettos. She perched coquettishly on the edge of the stool. Her face dropped as Mike staggered over to her from the bar. He wiped both hands on his trousers, and his mouth with his sleeve. He approached her stealthily, his elbows sticking out from his body on each side, like a man might approach a wild dog. She pointedly turned her head to the side to receive his kiss on her cheek. Next up was Pat; he walked shyly towards her, placed a hand on each shoulder and kissed her on both cheeks.

'I wish you the very best. I'm sorry we're losin' ya to a Latvian.'

'He's Russian.'

'Sure they're much of a muchness.'

Igor straightened up in his seat, craning to hear what was being said. Marty sauntered up to Stephanie and pulled her out for a quick jig around the room. Igor stood, looking alarmed. Marty winked at him as they passed. Josie announced a break in the proceedings and the women went to the bar for another drink.

Stephanie linked Carthage's arm as he leaned on the bar.

'So now, Carthage. You've missed your chance with me. How do you feel about that?'

He took a deep draw on his pint and walked away.

'Just who do you think ya are, Mr. God Almighty? I was talking to you. Don't just walk away when I'm talkin' to ya.' Her shoulder strap slipped and Igor moved swiftly to her side.

'Is this man a problem?'

'Naah. Feck him.' She turned back to Josie.

Carthage took up the pool cue and continued to play, ignoring Igor. Josie steered Stephanie back to her stool.

'Last chance, lads, we'll have three more kisses for the lovely Stephanie before she is lost forever into marriage.'

Igor stayed standing at the bar, his pint in his hand and his hooded eyes casing the room. The two young Bengali men stood and approached Stephanie. The first, in an ill-fitting suit and plastic shoes, pecked her cheek shyly and hurried back to his seat. His friend, in a linen suit, leather shoes and wearing a strong aftershave, kissed her on the lips and his right hand rested briefly on her breast. She craned into the kiss. Igor put down his pint slowly and bounded over. He grabbed his arm, twisted it then kicked him to the floor and started to kick him in the face and stomach. Stephanie staggered back, staring, fascinated in a disconnected way. Carthage intervened,

'It's enough. Back off. He's only a kid.'

Josie stepped between the two men, placing a hand on each arm as they stared hard at each other over the man on the floor, with nostrils flaring.

'Lads, lads, now let's all calm down. It's over. Back to your seats.'

Igor's two friends accompanied him back to his seat and to a fresh pint. Carthage and Josie helped the young man off the floor. He retrieved his glasses and dusted down his clothes. His left eye was swollen and he had a cut lip. He left the bar quickly with his friend.

The smell of wet leaves filled the room as Tariq opened the back door to change a keg. The hen-party, now just five women, sat around a table and the bar hushed as each took a turn to sing folk songs of love and loss. Igor and his two friends looked sombre, each alone in his world.

At the end of Josie's song, Tariq turned up the lights and opened the front door, and the atmosphere changed again. The street was shiny after a shower.

Stephanie stood at the door and hugged each of her friends as they left. Carthage sat at the end of the bar, watching Tariq clear up. Igor came out of the mens' toilets as Stephanie taunted,

'I never got my kiss from you. Will you not wish me luck?'

Carthage looked straight at her. 'Good luck.'

Then he turned in his stool to face the bar. Igor exchanged looks with his two friends and they left with Stephanie. Carthage swept the lounge as Tariq put glasses into the machine. Once finished he switched off the lights. They left by the front door.

Carthage heard a dull thud behind him as he placed his foot on the first step of the metal stairway. When he looked around, Tariq was on the ground being kicked by two men. He lunged to punch the nearest when he felt a blow to the side of his head. He heard a high-pitched hissing sound like a burst mains pipe as his body folded to the ground. Blood pumped from the severed artery, filling the space then expanding to compress his soft brain against the hard casing of his skull. The blood clot grew from the size of a bean to a tennis ball.

Carthage was sleeping curled up beside Marie, her head tucked under his chin, her shoulders against his chest, her back fitting the curve of his stomach, her buttocks against his groin, his member between her legs, at the point of entry, her hips encased by his hands, her thighs, knees and calves draped like a rug across his, her feet like two mackerel rolled in newspaper, between both of his. She was so cold, he couldn't warm her. He could hear Tariq calling him as a red canopy over the bed slowly closed them in. He wasn't leaving her, not now. The bed slowly lowered down a mine shaft into a cold damp pit.

What Happened

by BOB WHELAN

It was only after what happened happened and I gave up the drink that I realised I was fraida heights. A few hours ago – last night or this morning or whatever – I was looking up at the roof of *Paddy Fahy's* pub and membering how I skipped across the black slates on that job. I'm a roofer. As much as yah can be these days anyway. We do the bit of facia and soffitt as well, me and the brother together. Used to be me and him and the aul fella too but the mother made him pack it in once the back went out. The mother was like that. I think about the aul pair a fair bit now. There's things'll make yah do that.

I was standing outside *Fahy's* looking up at the roof and waiting for Angie. It must've been three in the morning. You'd always get a few late ones in *Fahy's*, specially on nights like that round Christmas. The pub's on Friary lane. One of the four lanes that run down off Church Street towards the Shannon the way water would. It's a grand spot, or so I used to think anyway, it's sorta hidden away between the terraces of narrow townhouses that look away from the river. It's a real drinker's pub. Before I gave up I'd be the first man inside in *Fahy's* and usually the last leaving it too. Nights like that night I'd be in early getting warm inside and glowing with the feeling of being someone new. I'd be thinking this could be a great one. But it wasn't always like that either. The weeks before what happened it'd been turning on me, sending me the other way – crying and that.

The lads were on to me earlier to come in. I won't tell them what happened. Won't tell Angie either. She's seven months pregnant now. She shouldn't be drinking and that's a fact. It was the lads who told me she was in there. She was sposed to be at her sisters. We'd one of our rows the day before what happened happened and she moved out again. They texted me saying, come in, everyone's here even Angie. It's not like I've been doing much sleeping since what happened anyway so I got up and walked into town. I don't mind the walking really. Don't think I could drive now even if I still had the van. When I got to *Fahy's* I couldn't trust myself to go in so I waited. I stood and watched the frost come down and settle on the rooftops.

I won't tell the aul fella what happened. The thing about being a father I suppose is you've only the one example. And I'd a good one. I was brought up the right way unlike half the younger ones these days. The one time I'd seen him drink he was telling the uncle he'd no happy memories of their father. I'd have to say the opposite. He was always warning me off the drink. Some nights he'd slip it in like we'd be watching the football – we both follow Liverpool – and he'd go, 'Your mother's worried bout yah,' or 'Your mother thinks you're losing weight'. And like that I'd see all the late night talking that led up to her making him say that.

You think you're only doing things to yourself, but whatever you do you do to the people who care about yah too. Sometimes they feel it worse. When I was younger I thought I'd everything figured out, but these days I'm thinking I was wrong about everything. It was my parents who'd the truth all along and they would've told me if I'd listened. They'd have told me family's the most important thing. I learned that one the hard way. I think I got worse after Mam died but I don't want to talk about that. I thought I was someway taking a step back behind the booze. I thought I'd figure everything out again and come out the better man for it. But things kept happening. It's like trying to trace out a moving picture. You're always behind. The worst of it is I regret everything. Not just what happened but the things that felt good at the time too. I wish I could go back and do it all again sober. See what difference that'd make.

I'd been waiting outside *Fahy's* for bout half an hour when the door opened. It splashed slices of pub light and beer smells across the cobbled lane. There was a woman inside laughing up from her stomach and she sounded like Angie. A fella came out – Dollar Dillon – one of Angie's exes, he plays music round the pubs in town. He smiled a drunk smile and held the door open for me.

'I'm waiting', I say.

He came over and leaned a hand on my shoulder. He goes 'I heard what happened. You're a lucky, lucky boy.'

And he heads up the hill toward the twinkling lights of Church Street. I smelled the beer off him and it made me dying for one. Dying for a drink's a bit like dying for a ride. It comes over yah in waves sorta til you can think of fuck-all else. I'd convince myself all I need is the one. The first one's always the best one anyways, that change from sober to something else. Even better I suppose when there's a night's worth ahead a yah.

Angie's a drinker too if I'm being honest with yah. Last time she was twisted she told me she thinks she members the night the baby happened. She thinks it was that hot day over the May Bank Holiday. You know how that is. Days like that yah start extra early. We sat out in our garden in the morning facing the backs of the next street of houses in the estate. Everything looked sharper and shinier against the blue of the sky. We drank straight through the afternoon and moved our chairs with the sunlight as the shade pushed it towards the garden fence. She told me later she went inside and got sick. Her skin shone in the sun. She was wearing a red bikini. One of the other people in the estate started strimming with a strimmer when it got cooler. It made a warm burr in the quiet evening. She kissed me on the lips as I was looking up at the bits of orange sky. We went upstairs and rode on the made bed with the curtains open letting the soft evening light fill up the room. When we finished she put my coat on and I got dressed and we sat in the dark garden and lit candles to keep the flies off. Someone in a bedroom facing us got dressed for bed under a yellow light and they pulled the curtains and their shadow turned the light off and left their house and our garden in the blue of summer night. We fell asleep out there and when we woke up the next morning around dawn time there was dew on the blades of grass and on the tips of our noses.

After waiting for an hour outside *Fahy's* I walked the few steps to look at the river which is like something the aul fella'd do. The water was cold and swirled like curls of hair over the weir wall and round the corner by the lit up shopping centre towards where the banks overflow and flood the yellow fields. I heard the sound of heels coming. The sky was bright purple the way it can be on freezing nights. A young one and a young lad sat on a bench by the river. She was wearing a short skirt and he lifted her leg below the knee when he kissed her. I've had my fair share of young ones down round here. I've given that up too.

It was in bed that she told me about it. We were drinking red wine and making red circles on the white sheets with our glasses. The rain was tinkling outside. She told me once she loved that sound. She's a strange one that way. She loves the sound of sirens too whenever they go circling the town after a fire or a car crash or a fight outside Supermac's on a Saturday night. She put her glass on the ground and said my name.

'Alan,' she goes like she was building up to say it, 'I'm pregnant.'

We talked for a while about this and that and what we'd have to do. I took the rest of the wine and splashed the red down the white sink. I said we should give up for the baby's sake at least. She agreed. But we didn't then and I didn't until after what happened and she hasn't yet. I suppose I went down to *Fahy's* to tell her to give up. I was coming into my ninth day off it, today's the ninth day now I suppose. The first few days being sober was better than being drunk. Everything seemed new. I'd go walking into town just to look at things. It's been getting harder though. It's hard sleeping and when I do all my dreams start different and finish up the same. There's always a car crash. There's always a mother and her baby.

What happened was we finished a job early. We'd nothing on til the next day so the brother fucked off home and I was in *Fahy's* for twelve. I used to love the early ones the best. Just yourself and a pint and the bits of dust floating in lines of sunlight from the window. The shut door keeping yah secret from the noise of the daytime ticking outside: traffic on Church Street, lads shouting from scaffolds or barrels being delivered maybe and later on the younger ones coming excited outa the Tech. It was a cold day like today – I mean yesterday – was. Everyone had red on their cheeks making their pale faces glow and they carried shopping bags with Christmas presents probably and puffed their breath out white with the effort.

I was fairly well on it by the evening but I thought I'd be sound to drive home. I stopped into Tesco's on the way for a few bottles of wine to tide me over til I fell asleep on the couch. Outside there was a choir of schoolgirls under the red electric TESCO sign singing *Joy to the World* up to the bare blue sky. I stopped and listened and left them a few quid when I started crying. What happened was I was coming out the road a few minutes from home. I was looking at the fields a bit. The grass looked hard and white like old paintbrush bristles. What happened was my van swerved, on ice I suppose, and crashed into a Yaris coming the other way. I was out of it for a few minutes in the upside down van. When I woke up I heard that song the girls were singing playing from somewhere. I heard a baby crying. I got out. The Yaris was crumpled up like a drank can. It was a strange thing. It was the Yaris radio that was blaring *Joy to the World*. There was a woman slumped over the wheel. I could smell rubber.

What happened was I opened her door and pulled her back from the wheel, to see. There was a cut on her forehead

sending red blood down over her white skin. I shook her –
nothing happened. I thought I heard sirens coming. I suppose
I did. I noticed the smell of drink off meself. Without a shadow
of doubt I was over the limit. There was a baby in a child seat
in the back. He stopped crying when I picked him up and
he wrapped his hand around my thumb. I'd never really held
a baby before. An ambulance came and a squad car came
behind them. They looked at the woman. I felt the cold for
the first time. I remember talking to God the way you would
when you were younger and making a deal with him that if he
let that woman live I'd change my life and do something good
with the rest of it. I knew the guard. Jim Leonard, the aul fella
knew him too and I suppose I was lucky for that. He looked at
my van and the car and whistled a bit. He stood close enough
to smell my breath.

'Have yah had a few?' he asked me.

'No.' I said.

I'm sure he heard my heart beating. An ambulance man
took the baby from me and brought him in the front of the
ambulance with him as they left for Ballinasloe Hospital. They
said all they thought she had was a concussion, that she'd be
alright when she woke up. Jim Leonard rang a taxi then to take
me home.

'You've had a warning here,' he said.

I knew by the way he said it that he knew what had
happened. I took the bottles of wine from my upturned van
and went home but couldn't drink them when I got there.
Later on he rang the house and said the woman'd be grand.
Then I gave up.

When Angie finally came outa *Fahy's* I kissed her eyes the way
she likes and closed mine so I could smell the drink off her
better.

'What are you doing here?' she asked like she'd just noticed
me.

'What are you doing drinking?' I go.

She gave me one of her looks. She walked away from me

up the hill towards the lights of Church Street. She rubbed her stomach with the palm of her hand.

'You should give up,' I go.

She stopped walking when she got to the top of the lane and sat down on a curb. There were no cars on Church Street. No taxis waiting in the rank either. I looked at the Christmas decorations hanging behind her in the shop windows. There were Christmas lights draped from one side of the street to the other. I know the lad who hung them for the council – handy number that. It looked liked we'd have to walk.

'If you still had the van ...' she goes.

'Yeah.'

'What happened?'

'I told you.'

'Not what people are saying.'

'Don't mind them.'

'Is what happened to your van why you gave up?'

'I gave up for the baby.'

I sat down beside her on the freezing curb. There was water bubbling in the drains underneath the street. I gave her my jacket. We could've been two teenagers after shifting in *Bozo's*.

'You're different I think since you gave up.'

'Yeah?'

'You're not as happy and sad as you used to be.'

A squad car stopped at our feet. It was Jim Leonard. He said he was on his way to close *Fahy's*. He said he'd bring us home first.

When we got to our estate Angie was asleep. There's forty houses in our estate but only eight of them have people living in them and there's twenty more marked out in the muck that they were going to build but aren't now. On our road there's only one other house. I suppose they'd think she's gone and called the guards on him again, if they looked out now. The empty houses don't look as new as they used to. There's something sad about them. One night I woke up and Angie wasn't in bed or in the house. This was just after we found out she was pregnant. I found her walking round the estate, looking in the windows at the not-so-new houses. I dunno what it meant.

When we got inside I lifted her – pregnant an all – into bed. I kissed her eyelids until she started snoring. It's me that can't sleep these days. They tell me writing helps. I couldn't say whether it does or not, but after she fell asleep I sat down at the desk in the corner of the room and wrote all this down. A bit of brightness is coming to the sky outside now. The rooftops are licked with white frost, the tops of cars too. When I'm up this late I start making promises to myself. Like, I won't ever drink again and I won't let Angie either. I'll go tell the aul fella what happened even though I never want him to know. I'll go to the doctor and see what damage I've done to meself. I'll go to that woman from the crash. I'll get her address from the insurance and I'll tell her what happened really. I'll get up tomorrow morning which is only an hour away and help the brother finish that job he's had to do on his own since what happened happened. I'll climb the scaffold no matter how fraid I am. I'll walk across the cold dark slates and be high up in the early morning. I'll look out over the whole town: the strings of rush hour traffic, the people walking to work, the school buses and the church steeple sticking up into the part of the sky that still belongs to the night. And when it gets dark and we've to finish up I'll go into that church and light a candle there for all the things I haven't lost.

The Final Flight of But-I-Am

by DARA Ó FOGHLÚ

When I was a boy I almost knew how to fly. Every morning in bed I'd practice with my legs lifted up in the air, trying to raise the rest of my body up too. With my eyes closed, I could swoosh around the town, arms out wide, grabbing handfuls of cloud and blue fistfuls of the sky above our house where I lived with Mammy, Daddy and my older brother.

One day, my brother said to me, 'Out of bed, lazybones, today we have to clean the house. Mammy and Daddy aren't well.'

'But I am learning to fly.'

My brother laughed, 'Little But-I-Am, you could spend the rest of your life in bed and you'll never know how to fly. You'll never be as light as a bird and you don't have any feathers.'

My brother's head was full to the brim with facts, but he'd only ever tell you things when it made you look stupid. My legs dropped onto the bed.

'You see, birds' bones are light and hollow, but your bones are dense. They're too heavy for flying, but just strong enough for housework.'

With each word I could feel my bones get heavier inside my arms and legs. Then I dragged myself out of bed and shuffled through every room in the house with the broom and dustpan.

One sunny morning, Mammy and Daddy never got out of bed.

'Are you learning to fly?' I asked them, tugging at Daddy's big toe. But they wouldn't answer. My brother told me they had already flown away, even though I could see them lying in bed pretending not to be there. After that, he made my sandwiches for school, until the day when I came home and all the food cabinets were open and empty. My brother took his face out of his hands and asked me what I wanted to be when I grew up.

'I don't know,' I said.

'Here.' He handed me a piece of paper. It said,

You can be anything you want to be.

'Now, what do you want to be when you grow up?'

'A bird,' I said.

His forehead covered over with squiggly lines and he began to write on another piece of paper. 'Take this. I want you to read both pieces of paper every day.'

The second piece of paper said,

Don't be stupid.

After that, my brother went away and never came back. He didn't pretend to fly away like Mammy and Daddy; he just got into an airplane that flew him to America. Its wings couldn't flap and it was much heavier than any bird I knew of, but it had four big engines that made it fly all the same. When he got off in America, they gave him a job. He sent me money in a letter that asked if I knew what I wanted to be yet.

I looked at the first piece of paper he gave me and thought about being a chess grandmaster, travelling the world with unbeatable tactics, winning tall trophies and golden medals wherever I went.

Then I looked at the second piece of paper and realised that it was a stupid idea because I didn't know how to play chess.

I wanted to be a samurai warrior who does not know the meaning of the word defeat, protecting the shogun and the people in his province. My sword would be the sharpest and fastest in all of Japan and every villain would fear the name of But-I-Am, the samurai.

Then I looked at the second piece of paper and realised it was a stupid idea because I didn't have a sword and I already knew what the word defeat meant. My brother told me it was when you realised life was a fight where you got beat up all the time.

I thought about working in the local shop, stocking massive pyramids of canned goods, sweeping the aisles so people could shop without getting their shoes dirty, and telling everyone to have a nice day as they left with their groceries.

I walked down to the shop where they told me I was very lucky and gave me a job.

I still read the two pieces of paper every day.

'Back to work, you eejit.' The manager was always saying. So I'd put the papers back in my trouser pocket and stack more cans of peas on top of the stockpile I had built. Eventually, it was a fifteen-foot-high pyramid, but the manager wanted them no more than six feet tall. He handed me a broom, and said,

'People don't want to see that many peas. You just keep the floor clean from now on.'

The floor was never really dirty anyway, but I walked the broom around the clean floor again and again, until it was so clean that there was not a single piece of dust left in the shop. I pushed it to the main entrance where I told everybody coming and going to have a good day but they didn't look like they were having a good day at all. They just bustled past with their trolleys, chattering into mobile phones or trying to scream louder than their children. After a while, I went back to reading the pieces of paper my brother gave me.

The manager's face appeared behind the paper again, as big as a blister. I don't think he cared if people had a good day or not, and I don't think he had ever had a nice day in his entire life. He was redder than usual and I thought he might pop. He didn't though. Instead, he snatched the papers out of my hands and tore them up. Then he told me I was fired.

'You're fired, dummy,' he said.

I gathered up as many of the shreds of paper as I could but some bits stuck to trolley wheels and other bits stuck to people's shoes, and they were all too busy to come back when

I asked them to.

'Sorrytoobusy,' they all said.

When I got home, I stuck the pieces I had back together with sticky-tape, but now they read,

Don't be anything.

And

You can be stupid.

I threw both of them away because I thought they were doing me more harm than good now. I wrote my brother a long letter telling him about losing my job and his words of advice. Then I went back to bed and waited for his reply.

I stayed in bed for a week before I got up to eat something. Then I went back to bed. In another week I got more food and left it beside my bed. I slept and only ate when I was really hungry. I became so bored that I listened to my breath coming in and going out just for something to do.

In ... Still no word from America ... *Out* ...

In ... What did he write on those two pieces of paper? ... *Out* ...

In ... What will become of me without my brother's good advice? ... *Out* ...

A long time passed. I ran out of things to think about so I stopped thinking about them at all. And then I forgot about them completely. I forgot everything my brother had told me, everything the manager had shouted at me. I even forgot about being a chess grandmaster or a fearless samurai. All I had to entertain myself was the sound of my own breath, so I listened to it come in and go out of me. In. Out. In. Out. All. Day. Long.

On the day I forgot the very last thing I ever knew, my legs got lighter as I breathed in, and my chest rose up as I breathed out. Then I did it again. I breathed in and my legs lifted up off the bed and when I breathed out the rest of my body lifted up too.

The engine inside my chest was just like the big engines on the airplanes that fly to America, so I floated out of my bedroom, down the stairs and exited the house up through the chimney just for fun. Up inside the sky, everything looked small, even my house which seemed really big when you had to live there on your own. I saw the manager outside the shop shouting through his red dot of a face. The boy standing in front of him was wearing my old uniform and looking down at his shoes.

I flew off then, stopping on the tip of the Eiffel Tower, and in a single leap I landed on top of the Taj Mahal. And then I went up into the sky like a rocket, through the clouds, grabbing handfuls and mouthfuls until I reached Russia where I saw the best chess player in the world. Then I flew to Japan where I saw great swordsmen training to be samurai, all trying to forget what the word 'defeat' meant.

I flew through the blue wedge of sky to where it turned black and blinked back at me with a million eyes. Below, I could see the backs of birds and airplanes struggling against the wind like ants in shifting sand. Finally, I ended up in America where I met my brother stacking a six-foot-tall pyramid of canned sweet corn.

'Hello there,' I said to him, floating above his head.

'Hello back,' he said. 'What are you?'

'I am your brother. Don't you recognise me?'

'You are not my brother. But-I-Am is three thousand miles away.'

'I flew here.'

'My brother cannot fly.'

'But I *can*.'

'Then you're not my brother.'

'But I am. What am I then, if I am not your little brother, But-I-Am?'

'You are too small to be an airplane.'

'I am not an airplane.'

'You don't have enough feathers to be a bird.'

'I am not a bird.'
'Then you are dead.'
'No brother, I remembered how to fly, that's all.'
'No. You are dead.'
'But I am alive. I am not dead.'
'Oh but you are, little brother.'